# Hans Benes

"Do we not all have one Father? Did not one God create us? Why do we profane the covenant of our ancestors by being unfaithful to one another?"

Malachi 2:10

"Return to me and I will return to you, says the Lord of hosts."

Malachi 3:7

"Awaken this soul, O Lord, from its material slumber to realize its Spiritual wonder."

Hans Benes (*The God Dichotomy: Letting Go*)

# Acknowledgments

No journey of the spirit is ever truly walked alone. Though the inward path is personal and often solitary, it is illuminated by the presence of those who walk alongside us, whether in word, wisdom, or unwavering love. As I look back on the unfolding of this work—*Believing, Becoming, Being*—I am filled with deep gratitude for the two people who have walked with me most closely on this path.

Thank you Dr. Vern Martin, for being both a compass and a steady light during moments when this journey became challenging. Your guidance was never about giving answers but rather about gently pointing me back in the right direction. You taught me that truth is not handed down—it is unveiled in stillness, in study, and in the courageous act of asking the deeper questions. Through your wisdom, I learned to trust the voice within me, and in doing so, I came to hear the Divine more clearly. This book would not have taken shape without the seeds you helped me plant, nor the soil of discipline and inquiry you encouraged me to cultivate. Taco Tuesday's will forever live in my heart.

And to my beloved wife, Jannette, your love has been the sanctuary where my spirit has rested, wrestled, and been renewed. Thank you for holding space for me—not just as a writer, but as a soul unfolding. Your quiet encouragement, your fierce belief in this work, and your patience in the face of long nights and unfinished thoughts have carried me more times than I can count. You have loved me into my own *Becoming.* In so many ways, this book is as much yours as it is mine, born of a shared life shaped by presence, purpose, and love.

This offering bears the fingerprints of you both. It is filled with your lessons, your knowing, and your continuing belief in me. May the words within it honor the gifts you've given me, and their energy drift outward in service to others who are finding their own path from belief to being.

With all my heart, thank you.

# Opening Prayer

O Divine Source of Light and Wisdom,

I come before you with a humble heart, seeking to awaken the Higher Self within me. I recognize that within me lies a reservoir of untapped potential, a source of boundless creativity and compassion, waiting to be unlocked for the betterment of this world.

Guide me, O Divine, on this journey of self-discovery and transformation. Illuminate my path with the radiance of your wisdom, so that I may see beyond the limitations of my ego and connect with the deeper, wiser part of my being.

Grant me the clarity to recognize my true purpose, the purpose that aligns with the greater good of humanity and the well being of our planet. Help me to understand the unique gifts and talents you have bestowed upon me, and inspire me to use them in service to others.

Fill my heart with love, empathy, and compassion. Let these qualities be the driving force behind my actions, so that I may touch the lives of those in need, uplift the downtrodden, and inspire positive change in the world.

Grant me the strength to overcome self-doubt and fear, for I know that with your guidance, I am capable of great things. Help me to rise above the challenges that may come my way, knowing that you are always by my side, offering support and encouragement.

Open my mind to new perspectives and ideas, that I may be a source of innovation and inspiration. Let me be a catalyst for positive transformation, both within myself and in the world around me.

May my actions be a reflection of the divine spark within me, a testament to the infinite potential that lies dormant in every soul. Empower me to create a better world, one filled with kindness, harmony, and a deep sense of interconnectedness.

I offer this prayer with gratitude and trust, knowing that as I awaken my Higher Self, I am contributing to the collective awakening of humanity. May my journey be guided by love, light, and the highest intentions.

Amen.

# Table of Contents


Introduction............................................................................1

Chapter 1 Who is God?........................................................15

Chapter 2 The Blue Pill or Red Pill?.................................27

Chapter 3 Humility and Silence.........................................37

Chapter 4 The Four Pillars of Divinity.............................48

Chapter 5 The Four Pillars of Divinity: Truth................52

Chapter 6 The Four Pillars of Divinity: Love.................65

Chapter 7 The Four Pillars of Divinity: Peace...............73

Chapter 8 The Four Pillars of Divinity-Joy....................80

Chapter 9 Choosing Your Path..........................................85

Chapter 10 I Believe............................................................96

Chapter 11 Here I Stand....................................................109

Chapter 12 The Cleansing.................................................119

Chapter 13 The Beatitudes................................................129

Chapter 14 The Transfiguration.......................................143

Chapter 15 A Day in the Life of Becoming....................151

Chapter 16 Living Prayer: A Map of Transcendence....161

Chapter 17 My Spiritual DNA..........................................177

Chapter 18 Salvation..........................................................185

Chapter 19 Coming Home.................................................197

Chapter 20 The Morontia Mansions................................206

Chapter 21 The No Thing...................................................218

# Introduction

*"The important Truth is that you are a spiritual being with the Allness of Infinite Mind within you. Whatever your needs may be, the answer is not to get God to give you more through some divine sleight-of-hand process, but rather to uncover and release your own "imprisoned splendor."*

Eric Butterworth

It has been stated many times, many ways: we are spiritual beings having a human experience. This truth, often repeated but rarely lived fully, lies at the cornerstone of my journey. *Believing, Becoming, Being* is not merely an account of beliefs and ideas but a means of spiritual transformation. It is the outpouring of a soul seeking truth, alignment, and ultimately, unity with the divine essence that breathes consciousness into all life. If you have found this book, then I trust you are on your own path of awakening. I welcome you as a fellow traveler.

This journey did not begin in a temple or church, it was born out of a life changing experience. It continued in silence, stirring a subtle anxiety that suggested there must be more to life than striving, surviving, and endlessly searching for fleeting moments of happiness. My path was shaped by the world around me, through the demands of modern society, the continued appeal of material success, and the subtle awareness that something essential was missing. These experiences created an internal conflict so intense that I could no longer ignore the call to search for who I truly am.

*Believing, Becoming, Being* emerged from the call of inner questions and the conflict between material illusion and spiritual insight. It was shaped by the writings and teachings of Ernest Holmes, Ralph Waldo Emerson, Thomas Troward, and Emma Curtis Hopkins. These spiritual explorers provided a framework through which I could begin to understand the unity of all life and the role of consciousness in shaping experience. But more importantly, their teachings offered me a way to move from mere intellectual belief to a conscious knowing.

The structure of this book follows the three phases of the spiritual journey as I experienced them: *Believing, Becoming,* and *Being*. Each phase is both distinct and overlapping, like the waves of the ocean rising from the same source and eventually returning to it. They are not linear steps but a spiral of awakening that intensifies over time. Spiritual growth, therefore, is nothing more than climbing the ladder of consciousness with each step signifying another level of spiritual awakening.

*Believing* is where we all must begin. In this phase, I challenged the domesticated beliefs that had come to define my material world. I examined doctrines, cultural narratives, and social expectations that I had embraced without question. Here, I came to understand the power of belief as the creator of my worldly experience. Through study, reflection, and prayer, I began to consciously choose beliefs that aligned with the deeper truths of Oneness, Love, and Infinite Intelligence. This was not a process of adding more ideas to my mind, but of stripping away the false clutter and making room for what was real. One must establish a foundational belief system before one can successfully embrace the inner truth such belief creates. This belief system is not a dogma but a tenet, a self-created principle of truth rather than an authoritative statement of belief expounded to be true by some organizational hierarchy.

*Becoming* is the embracing of belief and incorporating it into daily action. It is where theory meets practice and where the rubber of spirituality meets the road of daily life. In this section, I share how

I began to embody the principles I had come to believe. I practiced affirmative prayer, visualization, meditation, and the cultivation of spiritual qualities like gratitude, compassion, and forgiveness. I faced resistance from within and without. Doubts surfaced. Old patterns fought for survival. But with each conscious step, I experienced a shift. Life began to respond to me differently because I was showing up differently. The world outside started to reflect the change taking place within. The world was not changing, I was; I became the instrument of change.

This fundamental understanding eventually becomes a natural inclusion in an individual's lifestyle and value system, ultimately becoming a cornerstone of day-to-day living. The greatest difficulties one encounters are the potential clashes between external societal expectancies and one's inner held truth. How does one question their tangible world around them with intangible principles running contrary to all that is being taught and demanded? It is undoubtedly a difficult road the traverse.

At the end of this road lies a rainbow of bliss, happiness and love, a new truth, a new *Being*. Difficulties arise when the path to "awakening" requires the letting go of long established beliefs that have served you well in this material world. Rarely does this happen, with only a few known exceptions like Buddha and Jesus. This, to be sure, is impossible to attain without the required rise in consciousness.

*Being* is not a destination, it's awareness; it is the moment when we stop striving and realize we already are what we have been seeking. This phase is marked by an inner stillness, a universal awareness that surpasses human expectancies. Here, I found communion with the Divine not as a concept, but as a living Presence. I discovered my truth, where unconditional love and the peace that passes understanding created unbridled joy. This state of *Being* is not static. It is filled with life, with love, with the intelligence of the universe itself. It is the natural state of the awakened soul.

Throughout this journey, I have come to see the law of vibration as a key to understanding the mechanics of consciousness. Everything is energy, and energy is always in motion. Our thoughts, emotions, and beliefs produce frequencies that attract corresponding experiences. This is not a spiritual assumption, but a material reality. When I aligned my vibration with love, abundance, and unity, I witnessed miracles, not in the form of supernatural events, but in the quiet recognition of synchronicities, healings, and insights that revealed the perfection inherent in all things.

Consciousness is the field in which all this takes place. It is both the canvas and the artist, both the observer and the observed. As I deepened my awareness, I realized that consciousness is not something we possess but something we are. It is the universal principle that connects all beings and all things. In this recognition, the illusion of separation began to dissolve, and the experience of Universal Oneness became more than a theory. It became the foundation of my *Being*.

The energy of love is the current that flows through this entire book. Love is not just an emotion; it is a state of awareness, a frequency, a power that heals, unifies, and creates. In moments of clarity, I have felt this love not as something outside of me, but as my very nature. When I acted from love, I was in tune with the Divine. When I withheld love, I felt the pain caused by my spiritual disconnect. The path to enlightenment, as I have come to understand it, is the path of love.

This book is not meant to be dogmatic. I do not claim to have all the answers, nor do I believe there is one way to awaken. What I offer here is my story, my process, and the insights that arose along the way. I share them in the hope they will illuminate your own path, not replicate mine. Every spiritual journey is as unique as each soul undertaking it. But while our paths may differ, the destination is the same: the realization of our true nature and the remembrance of our Oneness with All That Is.

As you read, I invite you to engage with the material not just intellectually, but experientially. Reflect on your own beliefs, practices, and states of *Being*. Allow the words to be a mirror, a doorway, a catalyst. The power of transformation lies not in the reading but in the living.

*Believing, Becoming, Being* is an invitation to seek your own divinity. It is a call to remember who you are beneath the layers of conditioning and fear. It is a love letter to the soul, a hymn to the Infinite, and a guide for the times when the way forward seems unclear.

May this book meet you where you are and walk with you as far as you are willing to go. May it awaken in you the knowing that you are not separate, not alone, and not broken. You are a spark of the Divine, an expression of the One, and a unique note in the orchestra of Divine Truth.

Welcome to the journey.

With love and light,

Hans Benes

# Here I Stand

Here I stand,
On the precipice of greatness,
Where riches and fame and notoriety await.
All it takes is a step.
But here I stand,
Entrenched.
Entrenched in a life of need and fear.
Entrenched in beliefs and values not my own.
Where hope of escape, escapes me,
Where hope of change is a long, lost dream,
Of sugar plums and gifts long replaced
By the needs, of every day living.
Where making money is a judgment
Of success;
Where philanthropy is a sign of compassion
And spirituality.
Yes, here I stand filled with emotions
Urging me forward to an unknown place,
Not one established by a society blinded
By eons of messages of worthlessness and subservience.

Yet, here I stand,
On the precipice of greatness;
Do I dare to follow my heart
In directions unknown,
Through hills and valleys filled with burdens
Where greatness is measured by strength of heart?
Do I have the resolve, necessary

# BELIEVING BECOMING BEING

To become the next Lincoln or Gandhi or Buddha?
When my little sister says I stink?
Is it a self imposed doubt and fear of failure
That saps my courage and sense of adventure?

I close my eyes to dream the impossible dream.
And I hear Dr. Martin Luther King proclaim,
"I have a dream!"
It all begins with a vision,
An idea so easily dismissed.
But it lingers.
It stays within you night and day.
It says, "Yes! You can do it as have many before you."
It says, "Yes! You are just as good as any of them.
The only difference is they took that step."

So take that step!
Take that step so you may live and bask in the experience.
Take that step to erase all those doubts and fears,
Which have resided in the catacombs of your mind,
For far too long.
That next step you take
Will change your life!
You only need to decide whether it be forward or backward.
One step from the precipice of greatness;
Yes, here I stand!

*"And it is an important moment in your life when you discover for yourself the great Truth that things may happen around you, and things may happen to you, but the only things which really count are the things that happen in you...There is a great idea that you will encounter again and again on your quest: you are a living magnet, constantly drawing to you the things, the people, and the circumstances which are in accord with your thoughts."*

Butterworth

# Believing

*"The coming to consciousness is not a discovery of some new thing; it is a long and painful return to that which has always been."*

Helen Luke

# Chapter 1

## Who is God?

*"We are slowed down sound and light waves, a walking bundle of frequencies tuned into the music of the cosmos, we are souls dressed up in sacred biochemical garments, and our bodies are the instruments through which our souls play their music."*

Albert Einstein

"Malachi, who is God?"

"God is not a 'Who,' Hans. A better question to ask is, 'What is God' or 'why is God?' Or, perhaps, the most important question to ask is 'who am I?'"

I sat in silence taking in my Spiritual Guide's latest insight as I continued my struggles with the whole concept of a Deity I was attempting to understand. While Malachi's spiritual place, filled with natural wonders, where a mini waterfall provided the calming effect necessary to reach within oneself to feel the essence of All That Is, I was still awakening to my Spiritual Truth. Surrounding flowers of purple and yellow and red hosting butterflies and hummingbirds, added to the serenity.

"Before you can get to know God," Malachi continued, "you need to know who you are. How can you know God if you don't know or understand who you are?"

"I'm a physical person living in a physical universe."

"And you're attempting to understand a Spiritual Deity?" Malachi replied before continuing, "Remember your own truth!"

"What truth?"

"Hans, you must remember. There is no science..."

"...that can identify God, there's no philosophy that can define God. God cannot be explained, He can only be experienced," I interrupted.

"Correct! Apparently it's a truth you continue to forget."

"So, how does knowing who I am help me to understand God?"

"You are an expression of God personified. God is experiencing through you! It has to be that way since you are part of the Oneness, the Omnipresence. What you continue to keep embracing is your idea of separation from God. Until you realize and understand and welcome the God center within yourself, you will continue to struggle with the understanding of, not only, who you are, but the concept of Universal Oneness as well. Before you can move forward to enlightenment you have to let go of the idea of separation. God's Love can never be fully embraced while one continues to hold on to the belief that their reality is physical, not spiritual."

Sitting in silence, I attempted to let Malachi's words resonate deep within me. "Am I to understand that as long as I maintain a hold of my physical world, I can never truly embrace the Love of God?"

"It's called letting go! You wrote a book about it in your God Dichotomy books, remember?"

My cheeks must have turned a bright crimson as I sheepishly acknowledged my guide. "Why do I continue to fall off the ledge?" I asked, totally perplexed.

Malachi was quick to reply, "Because you don't fully grasp the process."

"I didn't realize there was a process. I thought that letting go and embracing God was the process."

"*Believing, Becoming and Being,*" Malachi emphasized, "that is your process. One is dependent on the other and no steps can be taken until the prior step is fully understood, acknowledged and embraced. One cannot become until one fully believes, and one cannot be until one fully becomes."

"There are no shortcuts?"

"Shortcuts never get the job done because they fail to immerse one totally in the task ahead. This is the reason you continue to struggle, Hans."

"Can I, therefore, assume my brief experience of '*Being*' didn't last because I hadn't fully completed the task of *Becoming*?"

"Back up another step, Hans. You haven't completed the *Believing* process yet," Malachi corrected.

"But I believe in and embrace the God within," I protested.

"Yes, you do. But it's fleeting. It comes and goes. Your belief hasn't taken root because you let outside distractions disengage you from the Oneness. Your primary focus, or, should I say, your perceived reality of the physical world continues to foster your separation. Until you fully believe that God is Universal and your reality is Spirit, you can never totally experience the unconditional Love, which is God. *Believing*, as I'm hoping you're beginning to see, is the cornerstone to *Becoming* and *Being*. You've been building a house of cards. It's time to build your internal belief system on bedrock, which can't be shaken. For once you fully believe, your journey to '*Becoming*' won't falter, and, better yet, '*Being*' is almost assured."

"*Believing*, if I understand it correctly, is the prerequisite to *Becoming* and *Being*?"

"Correct, Hans! But believing, in and of itself, is not enough. Believing and embracing the Love of God requires letting go of your material, illusionary reality and coming home to where you belong."

"Malachi, I'm assuming you're referring to my awakening to who I really am."

"Bingo! As Neale Donald Walsch stated in his first *Conversations With God* book, 'You cannot know God until you've stopped telling yourself that you already know God. You cannot hear God until you stop thinking that you've already heard God. (God) cannot tell you (His) Truth until you stop telling (Him) yours.' Let go of what others say about God and listen to what resonates within."

I watched as Malachi paused and rubbed his chin to gather his thoughts. I knew what he had to say was important and he wanted to make sure I understood. After a minute he continued. "Several pages later he states, and this is important, 'God does not reveal God-self to God-self from or through outward observation, but through inward experience. And when inward experience has revealed God-self, outward observation is not necessary. And if outward observation is necessary, inward experience is not possible.' Does that make sense to you, Hans?"

"It does. God does not announce His/Her presence to the world through a giant megaphone so that everyone is able to hear His/Her message. Instead, God's messages come from within and only those who have the proper belief system are able to hear and understand Him/Her."

"That's pretty close, Hans. But it's not a belief system as you call it; it's called Truth. When God speaks, or better yet, reveals Himself/ Herself, there can never be any question as to the intent of the message, for His/Her messages are always coming from a place of Love and are always centered on Truth."

"Didn't Neale Donald Walsch also say something about the trinity of Joy, Truth and Love?"

"Yes he did, Hans. He stated, and I quote, 'The Highest Thought is always that thought which contains Joy. The Clearest Words are those words, which contain Truth. The Grandest Feeling is that feeling which you call Love.' You cannot have one without the others. Love, Truth an Joy are inseparable because they are dependent on one another, just like *Believing* (Truth), *Becoming* (Joy) and *Being* (Love)."

"They are pre-requisites, one dependent upon the other?" I asked.

"Not pre-requisites," Malachi replied, "one is not dependent on the other, but they are integral to one another; neither Truth, Love nor Joy can exist apart by itself. You either have all three, or you have none, for they are the essence of God and God is always whole and complete, the Divine is never partial. The secret lies with the strength or conviction, or degree, of your *Believing*, which determines your passion of *Becoming*, which, in turn, determines your state of *Being*."

I could tell my visit with Malachi was coming to an end as he was staring out into space without uttering a word as his face became more radiant and light began to surround his essence. He turned to face me and smiled. "Don't worry, you'll get there; everyone eventually will. You can only deny who you are for so long! Remember how far you've come, go back to the beginning and give yourself some credit." One final hug and I was standing by myself, with more questions than when I began.

**************

Teacher's presence always makes itself known well before his arrival. The love energy radiating from his soul acts like a buffer diffusing all negative forces, which he might encounter. At the same time, his love embraces everything around him lifting it to an indescribable, euphoric joy. I always look forward to his presence beside me on our marble bench.

"Hi Hans, it's good to see you again," came his telepathic greeting, moments before his actual arrival.

"Hello Teacher, it's always good to see you. The love you bring always lifts me to unimaginable heights."

"Then we must work on making it permanent. Every moment spent basking in the unconditional Love of God is one less moment spent in the purgatory of material idealism."

"What do you mean?"

"Your objective reality is the propaganda that continues to feed your physical needs while failing to open the door to your spiritual home. You, mankind, has created quite a conundrum for itself."

"How so?"

"You want to know who you really are, while being afraid to let go of what you're not. Mankind has managed to position itself in a catch-22 that threatens to continually increase your dependency on this material illusion you call home."

"Then how do we rescue ourselves from this self-created hell we call every-day life?" I asked.

"I believe Malachi already gave you the roadmap to eternal enlightenment: *Believing, Becoming, Being*."

"Yes, he did mention it to me. He also informed me that I need to fully understand and embrace who I really am before I can truly get to know who I am. I need to stop vacillating between my material and spiritual selves."

"It's very interesting you should put it that way."

"Please explain, Teacher."

"By vacillating between your material and spiritual selves, you're acknowledging your separation from God. And by doing so you will never come to know who you really are. You may get a glimpse here and there, but you'll never be fully immersed in the experience."

"How can I rectify this?" I asked.

"In the book *We Consciousness*, Karen Noe presents 33 concepts of universal awareness designed to raise individual vibration to understand universal truths for you to disseminate throughout your worldly kingdom. Here are some of her more important concepts to apply in your life:

'Concept 1: The most important truth is that we are all one. Our oneness encompasses everything and everyone, including God, the angels, ascended masters, enlightened beings from other areas in the universe, deceased loved ones, animals, and nature.

Concept 3: The true essence of who you are is God. To say it in a different way, God is within every one of us - with no exceptions.

Concept 5: God is only love and peace; you must be love and peace to fully feel your connection with Him.

Concept 8: Our individual bodies create the illusion of separation from the whole.

Concept 10: It is imperative to focus on what is right in the world, instead of what is wrong.

Concept 13: You are an infinite spiritual being having a temporary human experience on this planet.

Concept 18: Forgive and ask for forgiveness. When you forgive others, you forgive yourself.

Concept 26: In order to live true inner peace, you must live joyfully in the present moment.

Concept 28: Problems cannot be solved with the same energy that produced them.

Concept 31: Your true life's mission is to spread the love that you are.

Concept 32: It is in giving that you receive.'

"This list might seem long and its goals difficult to achieve, but you must remember if you come from a place of love most things will generally work out for the best. As you stated in your first book, 'So you want to experience God? It's quite simple, really. Do good and be good in everything you say and do, without exception.' Instead of memorizing a long list of concepts, just do good and be good."

"In everything I say and do."

"Correct! And you'll find once these principles are ingrained in your psyche you will have completed the path of *Believing* and you'll be well on your way of *Becoming*. Go back to the beginning as Malachi suggested and you'll realize how much you've grown." Having completed his telepathic message, Teacher arose, pulled me into his aura and filled me with peace and love that lingered well after he was gone.

**********

For me, spiritual messages come in many strange and unorthodox ways. If one is not alert, they can easily pass one by as meaningless thoughts having no meaning. Over the course of time, I have come to know when a thought, a sign or a happenstance was more than it appeared to be. At this point, I recognize both Teacher's and Malachi's attempts to contact me.

The alarm clock read 5:15 when I was awakened by an urge to use the bathroom. As I was stumbling back to bed, "All Things God" and "Evergreen" popped into my mind. The message was an obvious call from Malachi to visit his store in Evergreen. I was thankful there were no subsequent messages requiring written reminders. Remembering more than one thing was nearly impossible at such an early hour.

Fortunately, my calendar was clear and after a hearty breakfast of waffles, sausages and tea, I filled the Camry's gas tank and headed to I-70 and Evergreen. Surrounded by tall evergreens, wildflowers and an abundance of wildlife, Evergreen Lake was always a quiet, tranquil and energizing place to visit. This time I chose not to linger and bask in the scene where I had taken numerous photographs.

Parking in this small mountain towns can be challenging, but not today. Malachi, I was convinced, made sure the F-150 pick-up vacated its parking spot just as I approached. Walking along the town's wooden sidewalk, I turned right on Douglas Park Road and my destination of "All Things God." Its logo consisting of a circle of people holding hands around a red heart whose point neatly fit into the center of the purple infinity sign below, was still emblazoned on the large picture window facing the street. Approaching the store, I began to smile, knowing my friend Malachi was waiting for me inside. A sharp "cling" announced my arrival as I slowly closed the door behind me. I looked around in disbelief.

"All Things God" was known for its rustic and tranquil atmosphere combining elements of mysticism, nature and spirituality, which were all missing today. Replaced by chipping, white gloss latex, gone were the earth tones of browns and soft greens and deep purple. Spiritual artwork, filling the walls, was nowhere to be seen. Normally filled with scents of essential oils and incense, the odors were more pungent and instead of enhancing one's relaxed state created an uneasy state of mind. Shelves filled with crystals, spiritual books and stones surrounding artifacts geared towards the many tourists strolling along the "Boardwalk," were not only empty but gone completely. Music from a Native American's flute no longer descended from the speakers.

Empty! Except for a metal white board standing where shelves of trinkets had stood not too long ago, everything I had come to know about "All Things God" was gone. I looked around in disbelief when a familiar voice echoed through my ears, "Hi, come on in Hans." It was Malachi as peaceful and loving as ever.

"Hi Malachi, " I stumbled, "what happened? The store is empty!"

"We're going to begin at the beginning without props, just a conscious exchange of energy filled with ideas, ideals and truths.

"This will be interesting," I replied.

"Yes it will. But it's necessary."

"How so?" I queried.

"Most people tend to travel the Spiritual road before they have a full grasp of what's required and, as a result, give up or get hopelessly lost in a sea of misinformation."

"Malachi, are you saying I am lost?"

"Somewhat. For what you have been shown you should have made greater Spiritual headway by now. But don't worry, Teacher and I will never abandon you nor any other man, woman or child walking this planet."

"OK, then, where do we start?"

"Have a seat and be prepared to listen."

I sat on the floor, leaning my back against a blank wall. "You have my full attention, Malachi."

As I settled in, Malachi picked up his marker from the whiteboard and began to write. When he was done, three simple words stood emblazoned in black against its white background, "*Believing, Becoming and Being.*"

"Three simple words," Malachi began, "with a world of difference in meaning and importance. If you truly want to reach enlightenment, Hans, this is your roadmap: *Believing, Becoming* and *Being*, each with its own path, yet each one is necessary to reach your goal. First you believe, then you become and then you be."

"Be what?"

"The I AM!" The road to enlightenment ends at I AM. It's the point where *Believing* has become knowing, *Becoming* is now a way of life and *Being* has evolved into a state of grace and glory. Another way of saying it is, Know it, Live it and Be it. What is your 'it' Hans?"

"I don't understand."

Malachi thought for a moment, stroking his white beard, before continuing, "Are you a physical being?"

"Yes."

"Is the physical world around you, your reality?"

"It has to be," I protested, "I live here."

"I know you do," Malachi answered before continuing, "so this physical world drives your actions or existence or being, however you want to put it?"

"I suppose. I'm not quite sure where you're going with this."

"What I'm trying to get at," Malachi began, "is simply this. What drives your *Being*? Is it the physical world or the realm of Spirit?"

"I think I know where you're going with this," I stated as a myriad of messages suddenly emerged within my mind. "This physical world drives my day to day activities; God makes an occasional appearance, but the issues of my physical world dictate what I should and need to do."

"And so it is with most people. As long as your physical world drives your actions, you have not yet let go. And, until you let go, you will never fully know your Divine Essence."

"Then how does one enter the Kingdom?"

"Everyone does! Eventually!"

"Is this where our lesson ends, Malachi? Will Teacher complete the lesson?"

"It seems like a good place to stop. And yes, Hans, Teacher will finish this lesson, if you want to call it that. My words of choice would have been to elevate your consciousness through awareness."

"If I understand you correctly, Malachi, there are no lessons because everything is already known. Therefore, all I need to do is re-member, as Neale Donald Walsch would say, and that is becoming aware of who I really am."

"You're coming home is nothing more than you awakening from a deep sleep and leaving your dream world behind."

"As Goldsmith would say, 'It is. It all already is!'"

"Correct Hans. Now close your eyes, take a deep breath and go visit Teacher. I'm sure he's looking forward to seeing you again."

*********

When I opened my eyes I found myself on that familiar white, marble bench awaiting the appearance of Teacher. As usual, his energy arrived well before his essence did, allowing me time to draw his energy within myself, growing and basking in the Oneness. My question was already formulated before he made his presence known, "Teacher, is it true everyone will eventually return to who they really are?"

"Yes Hans, that's true."

"Then why should we go through the suffering of letting go when the outcome has been pre-determined?"

"You don't have to, you have freedom of choice. You can wander in the wilderness for however long you want."

"Wilderness?"

"Yes wilderness. That's where you are right now, the wilderness."

"What is the wilderness, Teacher?"

"Any place where Love is not, Hans."

"So we can wander the wilderness for eternity if we so choose?'

"That's correct, Hans. But why would you want to?"

"Because we don't know any better?"

"But you will know better. That's why you have a life review when you transition. There you will realize what life without Love is really like."

"You mean when we die?"

"You don't die, you transition to a higher consciousness. You can never die because the Almighty is eternal and you are an expression of It."

"There is no death, Teacher?"

"No. As Rabbi Cooper in *God Is a Verb* states, 'death is a resurrection to a higher consciousness and vibration.' The body falls away because it cannot exist at such a vibratory level. But your real essence, your soul's consciousness is eternal. This awareness escapes you as long as you remain entrenched at the level of ego. Your ego maintains its focus on your perceived material reality, thereby keeping you chained to a world of need and issues. The ego's hold on the material world keeps you chained to a visible reality masking the Light of your Spiritual Self."

"So, how do I let go of the ego, Teacher?"

"You must understand that letting go of the ego creates a conscious void in your being that needs to be filled. You cannot let the ego go indiscriminately and hope it's replaced with spirituality. A solid foundation of knowing who you really are is required before a spiritual resurrection is possible."

"Why do you call it a resurrection, Teacher?"

"Because you're returning to who you really are, your Spiritual Self."

I let Teacher's word sink in for quite a while, unsure how to proceed or even how I got here. What I believed was a solid spiritual foundation appeared to be no more than wishful thinking. "Then let's get started on my spiritual resurrection!"

"Good Hans, let's get started."

# Chapter 2

## The Blue Pill or Red Pill?

*"Practically the whole human race is hypnotized because it thinks what somebody else told it to think."*

Ernest Holmes

I believed in nothing!

Nothing spiritual that is. Life lay before me with all of its nuances, requirements and obstacles. It was difficult enough to survive in a day-to-day world that offered little and threw obstacles in people's direction on a continual basis. Solving the daily riddles of life left little time for introspection or spirituality.

There was a God, or so I was told, who watched over us to make sure we behaved and stayed out of trouble. He was a God of punishment and expectancies and the further away this eight-year-old stayed, the safer I felt.

Prayer and meditation were not practiced in our quiet living quarters in Bremerhaven, Germany. Rebuilding from the war years was still going strong, as people lived wherever they could. Our family lived in three storage rooms atop a five-story building that was, for some reason spared from the allied bombs. The biting cold of winter and continual rainy days filtered through the roof directly into our abode. Our lone stove could barely keep its kitchen area warm, let alone the two bedrooms down the hall. Cold became a way of life infiltrating our bodies while hardening the heart.

But our family of four managed by scratching and clawing to

survive. My father steadfastly worked the passenger ships crossing the Atlantic from Europe to the Americas. While the pay was good, his lengthy absences from the family became difficult to bear. Work hard and good things will happen became the family mantra by which we lived. Prayer was not an answer to problems as six harsh years of war could attest.

My parents had risen from the level of Apathy (50) to a level of Desire (125) in a few short years. Hawkins defines these states of consciousness in the following way. "Desire, however, is a much higher state than Apathy or Grief. In order to 'get,' you have to first have the energy to 'want.' ...Want can start people on the road to achievement. Desire can, therefore, become a springboard to higher levels of consciousness." Without realizing it, my parents had begun to climb the consciousness ladder and, more importantly, had installed a basic belief system within me that would sustain me through much of my lifetime.

**********

"Teacher, I have a lot of difficulty explaining consciousness to others, can you help me with that?"

"You mean you have difficulty understanding it yourself."

"Yes Teacher, can you help me understand it?"

"Of course, consciousness is not easy to fathom. At its very basic meaning it's awareness, an awareness of self and an awareness of one's surroundings. Basically, understanding who you are. Are you with me so far, Hans?"

"So far, so good."

"Well, then you must also realize the fallacy in that awareness."

"How so?"

"Understanding who you are, in this physical world lays claim to separation, for the Divine is not of this world."

"So, explain it to me, please."

"Let's then start with the primordial force or energy known as the ethers. Within these ethers lies consciousness. Since these ethers exist all around us, it's our ability to access them, which determines our level of consciousness, or vibration. Everything vibrates, and the higher your vibration, the higher your consciousness.

"David Hawkins, in his book *Power vs. Force*, establishes a map of consciousness ranging from 20 to 1,000. Are you familiar with it?"

"Yes, I am."

"Then you must also be aware that most of the human world exists at level 200 or below?"

"I've heard of that, yes."

"So, what makes this level of consciousness so difficult to transcend?"

"I don't know Teacher, a shift in awareness?"

"That's true, but how does one become more aware?"

"I'm not sure, Teacher."

"Spirit! Spirit happens, Hans."

"How does Spirit happen?"

"By realizing that further conscious growth doesn't happen by holding on to your outside world, but to start going within. This is where 'letting go' happens."

"So, it's the journey within that transcends the physical world and opens one up to Spirit?"

"Correct Hans. But before you begin your inward journey something has to happen. Do you know what that is?"

"Letting go?"

"Letting go of what?"

"Letting go of my belief that my reality lies within the physical realm."

"Very good, Hans. You can only be conscious of what you're aware of and most people never internalize their being, hence they never fully realize the spiritual nature of things."

"You're talking about letting go of ego, correct?"

"Correct."

"Are you saying the highest level of consciousness one can attain is 1,000?"

"It is in your physical world."

"Why is that?"

"As your consciousness grows, your vibration increases. At the 1,000 level, your vibration becomes so high your physical body cannot survive it."

"Then, giving up the body is the ultimate letting go?"

"Correct! Don't forget, when you let go of the physical body, the ego will also disappear, as it cannot survive outside of its material existence. This, your final break with your physical world, therefore becomes your initial entry into your Spiritual one."

"So, consciousness survives the material world and continues to grow in the realm of Spirit?"

"It does Hans. There are many more levels of consciousness than just the 1,000 in Hawkins' model, which doesn't map consciousness at the Spiritual level. In fact, no man or woman can comprehend Spiritual Consciousness. It's far beyond their comprehensive capabilities. It's all enlightenment to you."

"Teacher, as one becomes more spiritual in the physical world, one's consciousness also increases."

"Yes."

"Is it safe to say that as your vibration increases, so does your consciousness?"

"Yes it is, Hans."

"Then how can we increase our vibration here in this world?"

"Let's start this way, we've already established your familiarity with Hawkins' model."

"Yes."

"Then you know it starts at level 20, shame, and ends at enlightenment, level 700 to 1,000."

"Yes Teacher, why doesn't it begin with zero?"

"While I can't speak for Hawkins, I can only tell you that zero consciousness does not exist, and the Divine always was, always is and always will be. Therefore, consciousness was never absent, but always present."

"That makes sense."

"Now, on the Hawkins map of consciousness, level 250 is considered neutral. Do you know what that means?"

"Not really, Teacher. But I'm assuming one's growth is more spiritual once the 250 level has been achieved."

"That's partially correct. As one lingers below the level of 250, the physical world, the ego, dominates your actions and beliefs. Your growth, or lack thereof, is determined by your mental activities of want, need, power, etc., in other words your growth is dominated by your mental activities. Once you reach the 250 level, the heart begins to get involved."

"If I'm correct Teacher, the mind can only take you so far. It's the heart which really raises one's Spiritual awareness."

"That's right Hans. Once you reach that level, the physical self begins to give way to a new spiritual Self; in essence, a new Hans is born."

"Like a resurrection?"

"Like a resurrection, Hans."

"Teacher, how can I raise my vibration through my daily living?"

"There are many things you can do, Hans. Start with knowingly wanting to raise your vibration. Let the Divine know you're ready, willing and able to embrace your spiritual Self. Then practice forgiveness, compassion and non-judgment, embracing a life of service, be grateful for all things, be present, monitor your thoughts, and engage in a life of prayer and meditation. These are a few."

"Basically do good, be good and think good in everything I say and do, without exception."

"That's it in a nutshell Hans, but simpler yet: follow your heart. Reiterating Hawkins, if you want to raise your consciousness above 250, one needs to move their view of life from the mind to the heart, from the ego to Spirit. Life is never about power, which resides in the mind, but about Love, which resides in the heart."

"So, who am I Teacher?"

"You are a physical demonstration of Divine Consciousness, Hans. The Divine experiences Itself by raising or lowering its vibration. Again, everything vibrates and anything can be experienced through changes in levels of vibration. In fact, the whole universe is available for you to be realized."

"Teacher, if I understand correctly are levels of vibration and consciousness the same thing?"

"Like everything else, consciousness vibrates; and as your consciousness changes, so does your vibration."

"Then Teacher, by combining levels of vibration and one's conscious awareness, it appears experiences can be unlimited."

"There are an infinite number of experiences available to you. All you need to do is to open yourself up to them."

"And that's through the heart?"

"Yes Hans, that's through the heart. Your mental factions are limited while the heart offers unlimited possibilities."

"Why is that?"

"The mind is limited by its environment. It cannot get past its sense of surroundings and needs and want, thereby blocking and limiting Divine Consciousness from entering. The heart can open itself freely without hindrance from the ego. Expressions through the heart are deeper, richer and more fulfilling. Creations originating in the heart become a mainstay of personality affecting many individuals and race consciousness in general. To learn how to create from the heart one has to overcome the ego, the king of your physical world. The mind (ego) controls; the heart surrenders.

"Is that the act of letting go, Teacher?"

"The ultimate letting go is to overcome the ego."

"What's the trick, Teacher?"

"There is no trick. Love Hans, Love is always the answer. Love eradicates all those things, beliefs and possessions and power, which stand in the way of your Oneness. Enter the Divine and you will never want, you will never judge, you will never be immersed in self-actualization. Enter the Divine and you will only know Love, Truth and Joy."

"Neale Donald Wasch?"

"Yes Hans. Neale Donald Walsch had his own conversations with God, just as you're having with Malachi and me. It happens when you open your heart to receive. Open your heart and receive the Divine, close your heart and receive the ups and downs of your physical reality. Notice, I called it your physical realty."

"Yes, but why Teacher?"

"Because your reality is Divine Oneness, which encompasses everything and everyone around you, including your physical presence. But your physical presence is only a small section of your overall Divine Reality. Everything that vibrates is connected to the Oneness. It's your conscious awareness of that Oneness that determines your reality at any particular point of Now. Let the heart dictate to the mind and not the other way around and you will never lack or want."

"Usually, I equate my heart's desire as what my heart wants."

"Desires are driven by the mind, Hans, strengthened by a persistent want of the ego. What originates from the heart is forgiveness, empathy, non-judgment, etc. These are the desires of the soul. It's a choice you make."

"I understand, Teacher."

"It's time to visit Malachi. I believe he can demonstrate it somewhat for you."

*************

"Pick one Hans!"

"One What?"

With that Malachi opened his hand revealing two small pills, one red and one blue. "Pick one Hans!"

I hesitated, not knowing what was going on or why I should choose one of the pills. "Why," I replied.

"Your spiritual journey begins here, by selecting one of these pills."

"Are we in the *Matrix* where each of these pills represents a different reality? One where we continue to exist in a dreamland of comfort under the control of someone's vision of societal norms?"

"That's the blue one," Malachi interrupted. "But if you want to awaken to your true reality by becoming aware of who you really are by letting go of society's expectancies, rules and regulations, then pick the red pill."

"What I hear you really saying is that I have to make a choice between material duality and spiritual oneness."

"Pretty good Hans. But the choice is a bit more complex than that. Choose the blue pill and you will remain in your material world of normalcy, unaware of your inner truth and continue to live your life according to societal norms. Choose the blue pill and you will realize the limited potential offered by a controlling and limiting power structure. By continuing to exist in your society's created Matrix, designed to keep you happy, yet ignorant, your true connection to Spirit will be stymied and could be lost for millennia."

"Malachi, are you saying that the world outside this so-called Matrix is more difficult?"

"Truth seekers always find the road more difficult, but much more rewarding."

"But why should that be, Malachi?"

"You'll be stepping outside the paradigm created for you, by following a path society isn't prepared for. The red pill represents a willingness to question and free yourself of the illusions created for you by the ego. The red pill will take you on a journey of self-discovery, transcending the limitations imposed by this material world. Spiritual Truth, by exposing the fallacies of the material world, is never an accepted path by those who have predetermined, and thusly defined, their material truth.

"Furthermore, the blue pill denies one the potential free will offers. Consciousness becomes stagnant when limitations and obstacles of a material ego hinder the investigative freedom required to search for Inner Truth."

"I understand what you're saying Malachi, but I'm sure spiritual growth can occur regardless of whichever pill I take."

"That is true, however, when material comforts and pursuits dominate the lifestyle, spirituality takes a backseat and is often overlooked or forgotten as the march for greater material comfort continues. Instead of opening oneself up to possibilities, people have a greater tendency to focus on success as defined by a materialistic society. Quite often, people with this mindset are more apt to adhere to created norms.

"On the other hand, individuals seeking their Truth by transcending materialism soon realize there is more to life than material substance and comfort. Soon after they begin to realize and, I might add, accept, the inter-connection of all things. Rationalizing through their critical thinking process they begin to raise their conscious awareness, which always leads to yet a higher consciousness. Breaking through the barriers created by society is critical to the conscious evolution of, not only the individual, but the entire world community as a whole."

"How does one come to the realization there is an existence beyond our physical world? Is it innate?"

"That's one possibility Hans. But most people begin to open themselves up to Spirit because of events happening in their lives, especially after the death of a loved one."

Malachi's statement stirred those painful memories stored in the darkest chambers of my mind. It was January 2, 2015 when everything changed. My dear son, John, decided to end his lifetime on this planet, leaving behind a grieving family and what appeared to be an unfinished life filled with promises of success and joy. Inner turmoil, I have learned, often terminates in tragic ways.

My son's death opened, not only emotional wounds, but caused me to look at the whole realm of spirituality. It opened my mind and closed my heart, begging the question, "Where was God?"

And so I began searching for what I wasn't initially sure, but it centered on the spiritual existence of God and my role, if any, in life. Dormant questions about the existence of the Divine, Its purpose and effect on people began to emerge. Answers came, but I was too busy, or angry, to listen. I hid within the catacombs of my mind, refusing to look beyond my self-inflicted pain.

Too many sleepless nights later, I began to calm my internal turmoil and seriously began to question the reality of things. I began to question the meaning of God, the purpose of God and, more importantly why this tragedy had to happen to my wonderful family and me. Slowly I began to open to the internal messages I had been ignoring for years.

"Give me the red pill," I demanded.

# Chapter 3

## Humility and Silence

*"A grateful heart is a beginning of greatness. It is an expression of humility. It is a foundation for the development of such virtues as prayer, faith, courage, contentment, happiness, love, and well-being."*

James E. Faust

I found myself sitting on a rock overlooking a mini waterfall whose rush of water, cascading over the edge and forming a clear pool at the bottom, sang a song of peace and tranquility, which resonated throughout my body. Its deep, peaceful feeling relaxed my entire body while heightening the senses. It was a place where the heart dictated the experience. I saw goldfish playing in the clear pool, while a short distance down the meandering stream I saw a doe with its two fawns quenching their thirst.

It was easy to get lost in this place, as nothing else mattered except this moment. I was lost in the Now. It wasn't long before another energy made its presence, one filled with knowing and wisdom. Malachi, I was sure, was on his way.

"Hello Hans how are you?"

"Malachi, it's good to see you. This place is magical. I can't imagine ever being in a more beautiful place than this."

"Oh, but you have."

"I don't recall. I'm sure this is the first time I've ever been here."

"My dear Hans, you've been here many times, but you don't

recognize it because this is the first time you brought your heart into the experience. The heart changes everything!"

"Yes Malachi, you're right."

"Since your heart is open to this moment, this might be a good time to talk about humility and silence."

"I would think love and peace would be more in tune with these surroundings."

"I understand you, but surely you must understand the underlying principles that are in play to enable you to bask in this experience?"

"I'm not quite sure Malachi, please explain yourself."

"Humility, simplicity and silence, three seemingly inconsequential energies, work in unison to bring you the heightened experiences of the heart."

"How so Malachi?"

"Humility serves to clear the clutter from your mind. The humble mind is devoid of want and need, it already knows what has been and will be provided. The humble mind doesn't get caught up in the daily power struggles and expectancies of a society constantly competing against one another. The humble mind is content within its own simplicity by not allowing outside influences to litter its existing peace. The humble mind allows one to fully let go and enter the silence."

"What is in the silence, Malachi?"

"All you ever wish to know! All you ever wish to know, Hans!"

"What does it mean?"

"The Indian mystic Osho, describes it this way:


'The energy of the whole has taken possession of you. You are possessed, you are no more, the whole is.

This moment, as the silence penetrates in you, you can understand the significance of it, because it is the same silence that Gautama Buddha experienced...

Time changes, the world goes on changing, but the experience of the silence, the joy of it, remains the same. That is the only thing you can rely upon, the only thing that never dies. It is the only thing that you can call your very being.'

I sat in silence, trying to disseminate what Malachi had just told me when he continued by saying, "Rabbi Cooper states the following in *God is a Verb*:

'My keeping silence was a means of building the sanctuary above and the sanctuary below. The sanctuaries above and below are the places where one has intimate ommunion with God...Here a new reality takes shape, one much more connected with the realms of higher awareness than is available to us in our normally noisy mental playing field. Here the small voice of God can be heard.'

"We've discussed the process of letting go before; well, this is the ultimate letting go because you cannot enter the silence while carrying any mindful baggage. It is the moment where the mind no longer exists; only the heart remains. It is the moment of pure clarity because only the Truth exists. It is the holy moment of individuality, which can only exist within the whole of All There Is.

"Close your eyes and clear you mind. Let me take you on a journey."

I did as Malachi requested and quickly found myself filled with inner peace and love, within soothing and embracing warmth. After several more breaths I found myself deep within the Self. "Open your heart and then open your eyes," I heard Malachi say.

Before me was total darkness. There was nothing to be seen. Was this the nothingness or no thing I had heard about? While nothing visible was present, the energy of Love and Peace and Joy danced all around me. I understood, everything was perfect; all was as it should be.

As I was basking in the Love a tiny pinhead of light appeared in the distance, instantly drawing my attention. Then another, and another! Before I knew it there were a hundred lights, then a thousand, then a million and then a billion lights all around me. "Stars," came to mind, "they must be stars."

I was in awe of the scene before me. It was as if I was on a mountaintop on the clearest of nights with a billion stars shining down on me. Only this time, I was on the inside looking out. Stars were everywhere, to the right of me, to the left of me, above me and below me. "Are you still with me Malachi? Are you seeing this as well? Where am I? What am I seeing?"

"This is your experience," I heard from a distance, "embrace it."

I continued to look around amazed at the multitude of stars before me. "They are not stars, these are galaxies," a voice came from within, instantly adding to the vastness of the experience. I was both outside of the universe looking in as well as being inside looking out, creating and living my own experience. I attempted to rationalize how all this came to be and realized this was beyond my level of comprehension when another message came from the depths of my soul, "Don't try to rationalize, embrace the experience. Let go."

Lights continued to emerge while others disappeared. I was witnessing a universal evolution right before me when a distant light began to flicker and draw my attention. "Take me there," I thought.

Instantly I found myself at the edge of a galaxy, travelling a billion light years with only a thought. It was a spiral galaxy with a vast dust cloud, the incubator of stars. It was the Milky Way. The loving peace I was experiencing was still there and I realized that all was perfect, just as it was meant to be. At the outer edge of one of its spiral arms a light began to flicker, calling me.

"I want to go there," I thought, and instantly I found my self at the edge of a solar system, travelling a million light years with only a thought. I recognized Pluto and the Kuiper Belt as I gradually moved towards the distant star at its center. I passed Neptune and Uranus, while stopping to admire the beauty and power of Saturn's rings. Next came the gas giant, Jupiter and its more than sixty moons. The red planet was next and from there I could see a distant blue and white orb with a singular moon in tow. Love and Peace and Joy were still with me as, again, I realized all was perfect, just as it should be.

Then I found myself just above the blue orb, having travelled millions of miles with just a thought. The loving joy within invited me down to the surface. I approached slowly, overcome by the planet's majesty and wonder, entering slowly through its atmosphere and coming to rest on a mountaintop. I could see for miles, as there was no pollution to obstruct my vision. Everything appeared to be in perfect unison and harmony. Everything was as it should be! I sat on a carpet of grass, immersed in the scene before me, realizing Love and Peace and Joy were still my companions. All was as it should be; everything was perfect. Out of the vast expanse of the universe, I found Earth, my home planet.

Coming down the mountain I saw a field of yellow flowers in the distance and knew it was my destination. I wound up on a hill overlooking a valley of sunflowers glowing in the sun for as far as the eye could see. It wasn't just a scene of beauty but a place of re-energizing and replenishing my personal energy.

A dim light appeared in the distance calling me to come down from the hill. While I didn't recognize it I began to feel its loving peace. As I reached the edge of the sunflowers I saw them open a pathway, inviting me in. Advancing deeper into the field, I began to recognize the force that was drawing me in. It was Teacher!

"Welcome to the Valley of Sunflowers, Hans."

"Teacher!" It was all I could say as I lost myself in his embrace, which might have lasted a second or a hundred years. I didn't know; it didn't matter. It wasn't really an embrace but an intertwining of personal energies, feeding off each other.

"Welcome to the silence, Hans"

"This is the silence?"

"This, or any other place you open your heart to. An open heart offers unlimited levels of experiences. Each experience raises your awareness and brings you closer to your Divine Self and the Universal Consciousness. The silence helps you to embrace and not control the experience. When you embrace you're at the center of what is happening around you; when you control, you're on the outside looking in.

"When you embrace, you activate all your senses at once. It's a total experience. When you attempt to exercise control, the experience becomes very limited and, often unrewarding. Always bring your heart and leave your controlling mind behind. With the heart every experience is total, never partial. The heart brings love and truth and joy and peace. This is only possible in the silence. What else could you want?"

"I hear you Teacher, and I think I understand."

"Listen to the sunflowers? Do you hear them?"

"I'm not sure, I don't think so."

"Listen with your heart, your ears are of no use here."

"Yes, I hear them. They're singing. I'm hearing them sing. They sound like the 'Stabat Mater' in all its glory"

"Their songs are expressing joy and love. In this field of sunflowers, there's not one unhappy flower. They work together to ensure every flower is successful, that every flower is equal. They realize that the least of them determines the level of success of the whole field. Sunflowers make sure every flower has access to the sunlight, there is no competition for more light. Likewise the roots share the nutrients provided underground. Not one flower uses more than it needs. The success of each flower contributes to the growth of the entire field."

"I understand, Teacher."

"Pick a flower, Hans."

"But won't it die, Teacher?"

"Nothing dies! As Rabbi Cooper states in *God is a Verb*, 'every death is a resurrection.' Consciousness changes, energy changes, vibrations change, but nothing ever dies because everything has its origin in Spirit; everything exists within the Eternal Oneness. When we're done with our finite being we return to our infinite Being."

"Because Spirit is our reality and we can never change that regardless how hard we try."

"Yes Hans. So take a flower, hold it, smell it, listen to it, and then feel its energy by holding it close to your heart."

I did as Teacher instructed. Picking up a nearby flower and holding its soft petals gently in my hand, I could feel its peace and love; I listened to its song of joy and oneness; I saw its aura and held it close to my heart. Two souls were melding, the flower's and mine. We were sharing our love, offering our peace and basking in our joy. I became sad when I realized this union was only temporary and the flower would wilt away soon.

"Don't be sad Hans. From its roots another flower will soon appear, while its changing energy and vibration has increased your awareness and joined the vibratory Oneness. Not many flowers get the opportunity to bond with another soul. While it may not seem like a big deal to you, the flower's purpose was to bring love, peace and joy into this world. You helped it to do just that."

Having said that, Teacher faded into the distance, leaving me standing holding my flower friend. With my flower friend close to my bosom, I quietly left the Valley of Sunflowers and made my way back up the hill. Sitting down I gave one final look at the sea of sunflowers and waved good-bye. I closed my eyes and embraced the peace and love my friend was still sending me.

By holding the sunflower to my heart, I breathed in, not only its love, but also all the love reverberating around me. When exhaling, I saw my breath dissipate while carrying my love to everything within reach, realizing as I was giving love so I was receiving love, and everything was working in perfect synchronicity, just as it was intended. Everything was perfect.

Subliminally, Teacher sent me one final message. "Each experience you enter fills all your senses and your heart, this is only possible in the silence when humility and simplicity eliminate outside intrusions. Spirit lives in the silence. Spirit thrives in the silence. Enter the silence and you will get to know your inner Self."

*********

I awoke when the enveloping warm, peaceful embrace left me. Teacher was gone and so were the sunflowers. Looking around I realized I had returned to Malachi's waterfall. "How was your journey, Hans?"

"It was unlike anything I have ever experienced. My body is still vibrating and my mind is trying to make sense of it all."

"Let go of the mind and listen to your body. The experience will not only last longer but will be much more meaningful and rewarding."

"How do I get back to the silence? How can I expand my experiences?"

"With humility and simplicity, Hans. Humility fosters selflessness and simplicity, which remove all the trappings of personality, including our desires, expectations and aspirations. In short, humility overcomes the needs of the ego, allowing you to see the world through greater spiritual filters. All of your great teachers had a humble nature; look at Jesus, Buddha and Gandhi. It was humility that made them great. It was humility that raised their awareness above all others.

"The humble person realizes there is nobody superior or inferior. Everything and everyone is equal. It is man's desire to be higher and better which leads to inner conflict. The humble person has let go of this inner conflict and is no longer interested in being superior. This person has come to see the Divine Energy in everything, while coming to the realization nothing is inconsequential; nothing is separated from the whole. Within humility lies strength, the strength of self-assurance, strength of knowing the Truth, the strength and power of Love and the happiness of eternal Joy. Humility allows you to see all this in your experiences.

"As Hawkins states, 'When you don't need fancy titles and money and all these other things, then you're no longer run by them, and you begin to value other things. You're able to love everyone, no matter what.' Remember, humility and simplicity will guide you into the silence where Truth, Love and Joy reside."

"Most people see humility as a weakness, not a strength."

"Yes Hans. Also, most people think that humility is fostered by fear when, instead, it takes tremendous strength and courage to be humble. Here, in our spiritual world, humility abounds. No one looks down on another. No one is expendable. Here Love reigns supreme. Remember what Nikola Tesla said, 'We are all one. Only egos, beliefs and fears separate us.' Humility and simplicity work in unison to minimize our egos, temper our beliefs and compromise our fears."

"Malachi, please explain to me how simplicity and humility help to create the silence I need to enter and continue my spiritual growth."

My Spirit Guide appeared deep in thought. I could tell he was formulating his response carefully to ensure its maximum impact without creating any confusion. When he began to speak, I listened intently. "These qualities have been the bedrock of ancient sages and prophets for over a thousand years, as they are regarded as the foundations for a purposeful and transformative spiritual journey, thereby holding the keys to unlocking the depths of our spiritual awakening. By embracing humility, we open ourselves to be teachable, acknowledge our limitations, and find compassion for the struggles of others who, we realize, are also on their spiritual quests.

"Humility encourages us to simplify our lives while focusing on what truly matters, thereby helping us access and experience the Self within. Through simplicity, we begin to understand that our spiritual journey will not be hindered by the burdens of material desires and endless wants.

"Spiritual silence presents us with the stillness and contemplative space allowing people to hear the loving whispers of the soul. In the depths of silence, we transcend the commotion of daily life and find ourselves in communion with our Divine Source. Connecting to this Source of Wisdom and Serenity helps one to elude the noise and distractions of the external world.

"By following these paths, one will come to understand the following:

1. Recognizing one's limitations, thereby fostering a sense of modesty, which prevents arrogance or personal pride.

2. Being open to learning from others, especially from spiritual mentors, religious texts, and diverse perspectives. The humble person is receptive to new insights and is willing to question their beliefs and be guided by insights from various sources.

3. Spiritual humility encourages respect and empathy for others' spiritual journeys and beliefs. It promotes the idea that each person's path is unique and worthy of consideration, even if it differs from one's own.

4. Simplicity often includes a deep sense of reverence and awe in the presence of the Divine and recognizes the vastness and mystery of the universe, encouraging a sense of oneness with all of creation

5. Humble individuals often feel called to serve and show compassion to others. They recognize their spiritual insights or experiences should lead to actions that benefit not only themselves but also the wider community or humanity as a whole.

6. Humility and simplicity include the willingness to forgive and let go of mistakes, both by the self and others, recognizing forgiveness and reconciliation are integral to the spiritual journey.

7. Silence is often associated with reducing the demands of the ego, including letting go of arrogance, pride, and the need to always be right, which can be significant obstacles to spiritual growth.

"These values pave the way for personal growth, inner transformation, and a deeper connection with the Divine, by creating an environment where individuals become more receptive to spiritual experiences and insights. While it may be expressed differently within various spiritual customs, the core concept of recognizing one's limitations and approaching the spiritual journey with an open heart and mind is a major aspect of spiritual humility."

"The process of letting go is not, at all, what I perceived it to be, Malachi. While it seems easier than letting go of possessions, in reality, you're letting go of the old you while embracing the new Self. It's a complete transformation of consciousness and truly is a resurrection to a higher Self."

"You are right, Hans. Entering the silence for inner discovery and self-reflection is a journey that takes time and patience. It is a journey leading to greater self-awareness, personal growth, and a deeper connection with your spirituality. It is also important to realize that within spiritual silence lies the ability to create an environment of inner peace, self-discovery, divine connection, and transformation. Whether through meditation, reflection, or simply being in quiet contemplation, silence is an effective tool capable of enriching one's spiritual journey while enhancing the experience of Divine connection. Embrace and believe the process with an open heart and mind, Hans, and allow the silence to reveal the treasures of your inner world. What you believe, you will perceive.

"One must, however, be aware in order to live a humble and simple lifestyle, one must have a firm grasp on their beliefs. Knowing who you are and what you stand for is paramount for the humble person. Humility is not for the faint of heart; it requires a strong foundational belief system that cannot be easily shaken. The road to enlightenment begins with a firm understanding and belief of who you really are. And that's where we will begin."

"And so it is, Malachi. Thank you!"

# Chapter 4

## The Four Pillars of Divinity

*"When we recognize Self as Presence, Peace is remembered, Love is expressed, Joy is experienced."*

David Howard

Today felt different!

After all of the discussions I have had with Malachi and Teacher, never had I felt at a crossroad. Malachi asked me to join him in Evergreen to start from the beginning. After all the conversations he, Teacher, and I have had, I felt I was further along the spiritual path than having to start all over again. Regardless of what I had learned and felt I fully understood, Malachi apparently felt a need that going a bit deeper was required.

I sat in the lone sofa chair in the middle of an empty room waiting for my Spiritual Guide to appear. It was unusual for him not to greet me as I entered. After a few minutes I began to close my eyes and entered the silence. My friend was waiting for me.

"Welcome to the silence Hans."

"Hello Malachi. This is certainly different."

"Within the silence spirituality is more easily understood, as there's less interference from the ego."

"I understand."

"We have spoken several times about numerous things, but today I want to introduce you to some new concepts."

"Yes Malachi, what are they?"

"First is Metanoia Consciousness."

"I don't know what that is."

"Basically it's what you have been trying to do as you began your journey in search of who you are."

"I still don't understand, Malachi."

"Metanoia Consciousness is a major shift in thinking."

"Like critical thinking?"

"It's more than that. It lies at the heart of change, a deep inner change required as one travels the road of spiritual awakening. At the core of this change lie the Four Pillars of Divinity."

"I have never heard of them."

"Truth, Love, Peace, and Joy. They are better understood in the silence, for to understand them requires one to know who they really are."

"We've spoken about that more than once. While I understand the concept I have not yet come to terms with the ideas of separation and Oneness."

"These are not ideas Hans, we're talking about reality."

"Of course, my apologies."

"Hans, to travel the path to enlightenment you have to know who you really are. Without knowing who you really are, enlightenment is nothing more than a pipe dream."

"And the four Pillars will help me get there?"

"They won't help you get there, they are the foundation of the enlightened."

"What are the Four Pillars again, Malachi?"

"Truth. Love. Peace. Joy."

"These are all concepts we have spoken about many times."

"Correct, but they are not concepts, they are the cornerstone of the enlightened. They are your true reality. Your understanding of who you really are begins here.

"Who are you Hans? What is your Truth?"

I looked at Malachi with a blank face, not really sure what to say or what he was asking of me. He seemed to sense my discomfort and continued without waiting for a reply.

"Truth is the I AM. Love is the energy of Truth. Peace embraces Love. Joy is the experience of Peace. It all begins by knowing your Truth."

"Knowing that I'm a spiritual being?"

"No Hans. Knowing that you are the I AM!"

"How do they work Malachi?"

"The Four Pillars of Divinity are not abstract concepts; they are the living forces embodying the very fabric of all that exists. They are the essence of what it means to live in harmony with the Divine. This harmony is available to everyone willing to listen and align with his/her Inner Soul. Hans, we will explore each pillar as a universal principle and a deeply personal practice. It is important to understand that enlightenment is impossible without knowing who you really are. You must also understand how they work together and are fundamental to *Believing, Becoming*, and *Being*."

"Are the Four Pillars of Divinity a new concept or belief?"

"Truth, Love, Peace, and Joy have been at the center of spiritual traditions around the world and the Universe for centuries. Central to the teachings of Ernest Holmes and Thomas Troward, their energy affects the very vibration in all things. As Holmes states, 'There is one mental law in the Universe, and where we use it, it becomes our law because we have individualized it.' The Four Pillars of Divinity form the basis of spiritual development as they are vital to formulating a solid belief system, which in turn grows the heart to practice that belief, while finally comingling with one's soul to be that belief."

"What about forgiveness, empathy, mindfulness, and brotherhood? The ideals being stressed from countless pulpits, which, in many cases, are driving human behavior."

"In spiritual traditions across the globe, from ancient times to the modern day philosophical works of Ernest Holmes and Thomas Troward, certain themes recur with striking consistency. Truth, Love, Peace, and Joy are not arbitrary selections; they represent the core vibrations of the Universe—qualities that transcend religious boundaries and cultural structures. Together, they form a holistic framework for spiritual development, addressing the intellect, the heart, the soul, and the experience of *Being*."

"*Believing, Becoming*, and *Being*."

"Correct Hans. You will find the Four Pillars form the basis of all human ideals and values. Let's begin with Truth, the primary pillar from which spiritual principles originate. While one can claim love, peace, and joy at any time or place, the spiritual principles of Love, Peace, and Joy can only have one meaning, and that meaning has to be centered on truth, not just any truth, Spiritual Truth."

"What is the difference then between human truth and Spiritual Truth, human love and Spiritual Love, human peace and Spiritual Peace, and human joy and Spiritual Joy, Malachi?"

"The difference is that one is conditional, while the other one is unconditional."

"Please explain conditional and unconditional."

"In the human world of form you love your spouse and children more than your neighbor. You claim peace lies in a signed agreement often coerced and defined by the winner of a certain conflict. You see joy as a temporary happiness triggered by some event. Do you understand what I'm saying?"

"I think so Malachi. We see the four pillars as temporary and limiting happenings in the course of daily living. They are not permanent."

"While that is correct, there's much more to it. The four pillars are unconditional, applying to everyone and everything. And once you embrace them in their unconditional nature then you must also realize that in your world the pillars are nothing more than judgments, for any ideal applied differently to one person and another is judgment. By accepting the unconditional nature of the four pillars you become aware of the universal Oneness of all things and beings."

"We are all brothers and have freedom of choice."

"Yes Hans. And those choices are always supported, never questioned, for at the core of any choice lie Love, Peace, and Joy."

# Chapter 5

## The Four Pillars of Divinity: Truth

*"Only the truth I give you here will save you: WE ARE ALL ONE."*
Neale Donald Walsch

"Look around Hans at what you see. Is that your truth?"

I gazed around a beautiful garden filled with aromatic flowers. Everything appeared to be perfect, not one thing was out of place. "I would have to say yes, Malachi. How can anything so beautiful be anything less than truth?"

"On the surface, I would agree with you, but what about what lies beneath the outward beauty you see here. Isn't there more to these flowers and trees than color and fragrance?"

"That seems logical Malachi. But what exactly are you referring to?"

"Isn't there more to you, Hans, than the reflection you see in the mirror. Don't you have feelings, emotions, and needs?"

"I do, and I'm sure so do the flowers and trees."

"Beneath it all, beneath the appearance of anything lies an energy, an energy which continues to drive the creative forces of everything you see."

"Are you saying there are multiple layers of reality, the physical and emotional?"

"There are not only multiple layers of reality, but you currently exist in them."

"Please explain Malachi, I think I understand, but I'm not quite sure."

"When you go out to hike in the woods by yourself, are you aware of the physical change that comes over you?"

"Yes, normally I enter nature a bit agitated or depressed, but after a while those feelings go away and a calm peace and serenity comes over me."

"That calmness and peace are energy, the underlying energy of all things. It is the energy of the Divine."

"So I'm actually existing on a physical plane and a plane of energy simultaneously?"

"There are actually more, but that's correct. The physical plane allows you to see and experience your creations. The physical plane is the further slowing of vibration while the emotional plane is a higher vibrational plane of feelings. So what plane, do you think, is your truth?"

"That's a hard question Malachi. I would think the things I see and touch. They have a tangible presence I can relate to."

"You may be able to relate to your tangible senses and what they bring into your consciousness, but how would you know what they are or what they mean without understanding their energy and how that energy is inherent within all things?"

"Is this energy the Omnipresence?"

"You can say that. Therefore everything you see and everything you hear and touch is the physical incarnation of Divine Energy."

"So within all that is exists the Divine Energy, which helped to create it."

"And don't forget, within that Divine Energy lie the four pillars of divinity, Truth, Love, Peace and Joy."

"What you're saying in essence Malachi is that the physical presence that surrounds us is surpassed by the feelings and emotions they create within us."

"Your physical reality, as you must realize is temporary, while your emotional reality is eternal. One has to be inferior to the other if only because one was created by the other. Understanding that what do you think your reality is?"

"The intangible reality where emotions and feelings reside."

"True, and wouldn't it make sense that energy would be longer lasting than anything tangible? Even to the point of being eternal or infinite?"

"That makes sense Malachi."

"Wouldn't you agree, therefore, that your Truth, as a matter of fact everyone's and anything's Truth, is that which has its origin in the realm or plane of the intangible?"

"It would appear so."

"Then your job is to return to your Divine Reality, and the first step in doing so is to realize your Truth."

"Who I truly am?"

"Who you truly are Hans."

As I again looked around the garden with its trees and flowers, it began to feel different. It was still beautiful and awe inspiring but slowly and surely I began to feel its energy. It was the underlying Love and Peace that began to build within me bringing about an unbridled Joy. Truth, Love, Peace and Joy, I began to realize are the cornerstones of all that exists.

"As long as you're searching for the Truth, you will walk towards the horizon, but never get there."

"What do you mean, Malachi?"

"Truth can only be known, it lies in a place where there is no horizon."

"You mean inside?"

"Yes. The search for Truth begins within. But before you go within you need to believe and have faith that you'll find your Truth there. Belief and faith are the stepping stones for the Truth seekers, they help give you direction but fall away once your Truth is realized. Here's what I mean:

| Belief is? | I don't know |
| Faith is?! | I think I know |
| Truth is! | I know |

"Remember, you can only know your Truth to the degree of your experience. If you haven't experienced something you can't know its Truth. You can think it, believe it, have faith in it, but you can't know it."

"Malachi, does that mean Truth never changes?"

"Yes Hans. Truth is the bedrock of all existence. It cannot be shaken by wind, rain, or heat. It cannot be changed by thoughts or wishes of the Truth seekers. Look at yourself in the mirror, do you see Truth? Look at yourself again tomorrow, will you see the same Truth or has it changed by a wrinkle or a loss of hair, or a change in demeanor? Remember, Truth never changes."

"So where do you find Truth, Malachi?"

"You can search for Truth in the world of form, but you'll find form changes from day to day, week to week, and month to month, eventually disintegrating into nothingness. The truth that was once Mars is nowhere to be found today. The truth that was your planet a millennium ago is not its truth today. The truth that was you a decade ago is not your truth today."

"So where do I find this elusive Truth that is the center of all existence, that is the cornerstone of who I am?"

"Hans, begin your search where you are not, for where you are not never changes, but you can also never know it as long as you're searching where you are. Begin by eliminating your distractions, close your eyes, cover your ears, pinch your nose, swallow your tongue, and fold your hands, and then hold your breath. Your Truth will appear to you, not as a tangible expression but as an intangible knowing.

"Truth never dies for it is! Anything that is, never changes, for it never will be or ever was! It has no future or past, it only exists in the glorious moment of Now!

"Holmes defines Truth this way:

'(Truth is) that which is. It is the Reason, Cause and Power in and through everything. It is Birthless, Deathless, Changeless, Complete, Perfect, Whole, Self-Existent,

Causeless, Almighty, God, Spirit, Law, Mind, Intelligence, and anything and everything that implies Reality.'"

"This is heavy stuff, Malachi."

"It is only heavy to the mind that has erased its conscious connection to Truth. Your truth changes from day to day as you meander from experience to experience, always thinking that today you will find it. But you continue searching for Truth in a world that is constantly changing. How can you search for something that never changes in a world built on continual change? You need to change the place where you search."

"Where is that, Malachi?"

"Where you are not!"

"How do I get there?"

"Thinking about it or imagining it won't get you there. It will always remain a dream that won't come true. You need to enter the place where all true creation takes place."

"What place is that?"

"The No-thing, the Nothingness."

"How do I get there?"

"Clear your mind of all debris that resides there, and once cleared, wait."

"Wait for what?"

"For Truth to appear!"

"How will I know?"

"You will see it, you will hear it, you will taste it, you will smell it, and you will touch it. In short, you will experience it!"

"There is no science that can identify God. There is no philosophy that can define God. God cannot be explained, God can only be experienced."

"Correct Hans. God is Truth and Truth is God. Everyone and everything that experiences God has the same experience for it is the experience of Truth. Once you experience Truth you will know God and you will know who you really are."

The time has come, the hour has struck.
The power from within has come forth and is expressing
through my word.
I do not have to wait; today is the time.
Today I enter into all Truth; today I am completely healed.
Today I enter into my inheritance.
*Today the Truth has made me free.*

Ernest Holmes


"I believe Teacher will have more to tell you about the pillar of Truth, Hans." With that being said, I closed my eyes and breathed deeply awaiting the appearance of my guide, Teacher."

***********

As expected, Teacher appeared out of nowhere, radiant as ever. His aura was a mixture of lavender, turquoise and green hues seemingly interacting as one glorious ebbing and flowing of Divine Energy. "I understand Malachi has introduced you to the Four Pillars of Divinity."

"Yes he has."

"And what is your initial reaction?"

"What feels good to me is that the pillars are Spiritual Truths aimed at incorporating behaviors which are designed to embrace spirituality."

"Well, they're not really designed for any specific purpose, they are, as you say, Spiritual Truths. And Spiritual Truths never die or change, they remain eternally unaltered. These four pillars are engrained in the vibrational energy of All That Is. Nothing more, nothing less."

"Will these Truths help me to awaken to my spiritual nature?"

"The Truths are not tools to help you realize or awaken to anything. They are Truths that the enlightened become aware of once they have discarded the coat of their physical nature. These Truths are not beliefs, they are the means of *Being*."

"What about forgiveness, empathy, and brotherhood, those ideals being consistently preached?"

"All of your ideals are incorporated within the four pillars. Let me explain. These pillars are not abstract principles; they are an absolute energy included in the vibration of Divine Being. They cannot be arbitrarily altered or ignored. These pillars are the bedrock of the great masters, Jesus, Buddha, and Krishna, to name a few."

"So how do I get to know these pillars, are there lessons to learn and follow?"

"There are no lessons to learn or follow, they are a means of *Being*. Truth is the first pillar because it lays the foundation of who you really are. It never changes and is not limited by space and time. Truth is the pathway to enlightenment, it is the recognition of what is, of who you really are."

"How does that differ from our truth in the realm of the physical Teacher?"

"As physical beings you are conditioned by your personal experiences, influenced by societal norms, and emotional responses, causing you to struggle in distinguishing Divine Truth from the truth you see in your physical reality. Over the course of time you have accepted your material truths, rarely questioning their validity or origin."

"So how do I find my Truth?"

"Let me see if I can put this simply Hans. There are several stages in searching for Truth. The first stage is to distinguish what is real and what is not. It is an analytical process, which challenges and investigates your physical reality for inconsistencies while seeking an internal clarity."

"What inconsistencies Teacher?"

"Those inconsistencies between what is being taught and what your internal judgments maintain, for example, the concept of God. There are numerous religions all believing in a deity based upon individual and collective needs, wants, and desires. Internally, however, the concept of a deity may vary greatly, placing greater emphasis on what is right or wrong; concepts that are not taught but 'feel' right."

"Are you saying that we need to go within to find our Truth?"

"Correct. The second stage is one of clarity. In this stage one needs to confront how fear and attachment obscure our perception of Truth. People have a tendency to embrace things of comfort or avoid uncomfortable situation, thereby allowing their emotions to dictate their behavior. By fostering self-awareness and emotional flexibility one begins to recognize these falsehoods thereby opening one up to their critical thinking prowess, opening themselves up to the voice within."

"Again, the secret is to go within? Right Teacher?"

"Yes Hans. The final stage is the realization of one's spirituality. Here Truth is no longer being sought; Truth is being experienced. Truth is no longer a concept but, instead, Truth is a living presence in constant contact with the Divine, a profound awareness encompassing all things."

"Teacher, what does living in Truth look like?"

"To live Truth is simply to embrace integrity while bringing clarity to every aspect of life. It means to act, speak and think in ways that reflect Divine Oneness. This alignment is an ongoing practice, a total commitment to honesty, humility and simplicity. The expression of Truth involves aligning your actions with your highest values. Pursuing Truth in this manner lays the path to spiritual liberation, which is a deeper more fulfilling interaction in every moment with every person."

"As the Bible says in John 8:32, 'You shall know the truth, and the truth shall set you free.'"

"That is exactly right, Hans."

"What exactly is Truth Teacher."

"Truth is that which is, that which can't be destroyed or harmed by any opposition, no matter how determined or powerful. Truth stands alone, never wavering, never changing. Truth simply is."

"So God is Truth?"

"God is Truth because he is unchanging and unaffected by events happening around Him. God has always been the energy of Love and will always continue to be so. God is Divine Spiritual Truth."

"If God is Spiritual Truth, is there such a thing as physical truth?"

"Of course Hans, but it's truth at a different level. Physical truth is temporary because all of physicality is temporary, changing from day to day and ultimately coming to an end. You can say that the temporary nature of physicality is one of its truths."

"I sense that there is a big difference between Spiritual Truth and physical truth, Teacher."

"Of course there is. One truth is eternal while the other is temporary. Physical truth exists within Spiritual Truth. It has to be that way because Spirituality begets physicality. It has to be that way because of Oneness. Here's a quote from *The Joy of Meditation*, by Jack and Cornelia Addington:

'...that vital moment when I was baptized by the Holy Spirit within. For one perfect second, unexpected, unheralded, and while I was doing a trivial task, my personal mind and body were fused in Light: a breathless, unbearable Light - Perfection as intense as the explosion of a flash of lightning within me... In this timeless second I knew a Love, Wisdom, Knowledge, and ecstasy transcending anything I could understand or describe. I was lifted into the midst of God in whom all people, all worlds, and every created life or thing moved and had their being. Perfection! Had I been suffering from the worst mental or physical disease known to man, in that Light I should instantly have been made Whole.'

"Imagine the power of Truth behind this experience, one instant, one moment of Now has the power to permanently change a person. The omnipotence of Divine Truth cannot be imagined."

"It can only be experienced."

"Yes Hans. All there is, all you see, and all you experience is embodied within this Divine Truth. That is your goal; that is what awakening is all about; that is your Truth."

"Teacher, I assume that Truth is the First Pillar of Divinity, the cornerstone, so to speak, from which the other pillars come into being."

"Truth is the essential principle, the bedrock, so to speak; without Truth awakening becomes impossible. Truth is not about facts and understanding, it is the recognition of what is. Truth is the light, which erases our doubts, the guide who lights our path, and the mirror that reflects our Divinity. Truth is absolute. It cannot be altered; it transcends space and time; it is never temporary, it is eternal."

"We see our truth through our senses and measure it by our ability to see and touch. We see truth as that which supports our physical existence and well-being."

"That's true Hans. Your truth is filtered by your perceptions, which are enhanced by your senses, your personal history, societal influences, and emotional prejudice."

"Teacher, I think you've clarified the enlightenment process for me. It seems like I had it backwards, that the enlightened path requires acceptance and forgiveness and gratitude. These were required so I could find my Spiritual Self, which ultimately led to Divine Truth. You're saying that Divine Truth is what we should be seeking and all the rest of it will follow naturally."

"Yes! Finding your Truth requires a willingness to question and courage to scrutinize the prevailing beliefs and assumptions that exist in today's society. This process unfolds in stages as you move from the truths of an external society to the internal Truth of Spiritual Reality."

"What are the stages Teacher?'

"The first stage can be described as developing an intellectual wisdom. Here you engage in rationalizing what is real and what is not. It involves seeking clarity, which is limited by thought and communication."

"I like to refer to this as the critical thinking process Teacher."

"That's very appropriate Hans. The second stage is seeking emotional clarity. Here one confronts their demons of fear, desires and attachments, which often cloud perceptions of reality. Developing self-awareness and emotional detachment helps one to see beyond their fears and desires, thereby gaining a better perspective of reality.

"The third stage is spiritual realization. Here one is no longer seeking Truth or attempting to understand it. Here Truth is something to be experienced. Through meditation and prayer we gain direct communication with our Divine Inner Self. Here Truth becomes a living presence, an awareness encompassing all things, embracing Oneness."

"If I have this correct Teacher. First one begins to question what has been established as truth in our physical world. Then we seek emotional stability by eliminating the fears and attachments that keep us from searching for Truth, thereby inhibiting our spiritual growth. And finally, once the first two stages have been attained, we are able to embrace our spirituality, where we'll find our Divine Truth."

"That's correct Hans. Once you're at the final stage, the illusion of truth disappears and the Universal Truth of all things comes into focus. It is here where enlightenment resides."

"Am I correct in stating that in order to attain Truth, I have to let go of truth?"

"Yes Hans. Quite a catch-22 isn't it?"

"I'll say."

"Then you must realize that the obstacles to Truth are self-inflicted. As you journey through life justifying your actions, needs, and emotions, you're actually imprisoning yourself with walls stronger than steel, your beliefs! The more you embrace your social construct the deeper imbedded you become in the illusion you call life."

"Our social conditioning, or domestication, begins at a very early age as we are taught how to act and socialize with others. We are burdened by expectancies on how to interact with others and we are even taught how to judge ourselves by comparing our achievements to others."

"Very true, but your domestication doesn't start at an early age, it begins as soon as your born."

"How so Teacher?"

"The ego! The ego is born at the same time your physical birth takes place. The cries of infancy are a cry for need. Now granted, at that stage it's very necessary for the ego to make your needs known. The ego continues its selfish march throughout your lifetime and, thereby, creating a greater division between you and your neighbor, between you and your Spirit."

"So Truth, if I'm correct, is the means of controlling the ego, minimizing its campaigns of fear, including change, lack, and the unknown."

"By walking the path of Truth, one begins to question established assumptions and impositions. Hans, the search for Truth is founded on the principles of integrity, empathy, and brotherhood in every aspect of life."

"Do good, be good, and think good in everything you say and do?"

"Simple and straight to the point Hans. It is a mantra one can invoke daily in every aspect of life. While it may be difficult to understand, Truth is the path to liberation, the path where spiritual awareness frees the soul. 'You shall know the truth, and the truth shall set you free.' (John 8:32) In Friendship With God, Neale Donald Walsch states, 'Each day you must make your decisions. Know only that, in deciding, you are announcing and demonstrating Who You Are...Every act is an act of self-definition.' Truth, therefore, is not something to be found, it's something to be demonstrated. Every day, every moment, and every instant you are demonstrating Who You Are. With each step, or action, you take the Truth of spiritual awareness unfolds itself."

"So each time I embrace Truth, I am letting go of ego?"

"That is correct Hans. Truth offers you Spiritual liberation and only asks for courage and humility in return."

"Teacher, am I right in understanding that Truth is the essence of the Divine? Without it Love, Peace and Joy cannot exist?"

"Yes. Truth is the path and destination, the question and the answer, it is personal and universal, it exists within and without, it is the no-thing and everything. It is the journey that leads to Who You Really

Are, Divine Essence. It is the foundational Pillar of Divinity upon which the pillars of Love, Peace and Joy are built."

"Thank you Teacher, this has been very insightful."

"Let me leave you with a quote from Ralph Waldo Emerson:

'To believe your own thought, to believe that what is true for you in your private heart is true for all men, - that is genius. Speak your latent conviction, and it shall be universal sense; for always the inmost becomes the outmost.'

He continues:

'It is no proof of a man's understanding to be able to affirm whatever he pleases; but to be able to discern that which is true is true, and that which is false is false, this is the mark and character of intelligence.'

# Chapter 6

## The Four Pillars of Divinity: Love

*"This is the Spirit of Infinite Love. The moment we recognize ourselves as one with it we become so filled with love that we see only the good in all."*

Ralph WaldoTrine

Love, the gentle flame that burns within,
Radiating warmth, dispelling darkness,
It knows no boundaries, no prejudice,
A force that has the power to heal and transform.

In the depths of love, compassion resides,
A balm for wounds, a salve for pain,
With open arms, it embraces the broken,
Mending the fractures, making us whole again.

Love speaks the language of unity,
Breaking down walls that divide,
It sees the shared humanity in every soul,
And beckons us to walk together, side by side.

Love is the seed from which kindness blooms,
A gentle touch, a tender word,
It ripples outwards, creating a wave,
Touching hearts, like songs that need to be heard.

Love in action is a beacon of hope,
A catalyst for change, both big and small,
It fuels the drive to serve and uplift,
To lend a hand, to answer the call.

Love moves mountains, bridges divides,
Bringing light where there was once despair,
It ignites the flame of empathy within us all,
And shows us how much we truly care.

In every act of love, a ripple begins,
Spreading far and wide, beyond our sight,
A symphony of kindness, echoing through time,
A testament to love's enduring might.

So let love guide us in all we do,
May it shape our thoughts and steer our way,
For when we let love serve the world,
We transform lives, we make a brighter day.

These days I'm meeting with Teacher and Malachi on a regular basis focusing not on forgiveness, acceptance, or judgment, but on embracing the Truth of who I really am. Instead of relying on individual traits to bring me to the Oneness, I'm focusing on knowing my Oneness, knowing the individual traits will become clear to me in the process.

I was sitting on the marble bench when I felt Teacher's energy approaching. His message arrived well before he did. "Love is universal, it is a state of being. If your love is focused on a single object or person it is an emotion, not the unconditional, all-encompassing Love of the Divine. The Love that emerges from Truth is an energy that sustains Divine Being. It is an energy that is shared with all beings and things. It is given freely and unconditionally and is returned to the same degree it is sent."

"Are we discussing the second Pillar of the Divine, Love?"

Without stopping to answer my question, Teacher continued, "Love does not play favorites; it does not elevate one person or thing over another. All are equal in the eyes of Love. It never wanes or falters. Within Love resides acceptance for it recognizes who you really are. Its energy peels away the physical facade and reveals the soul beneath. To truly Love in the physical sense, one must free the soul. Free it to express itself without restrictions for the expression of the soul is Divine Love.

"Since the soul is at the center of who you really are, it stands to reason that you are a being of Love. Just like Truth, Love is! Emerging from the Light that is God, Love is given freely and equally to all of God's expressions. It is the gift that surpasses all understanding."

"Teacher, is Love omnipresent?"

"Love is, Love always was, and Love always will be. Love exists in every corner of the Oneness. You can ignore it, but you can't escape it. Your ego looks for love where it does not exist, in your imaginary physical world you created. The Universal Divinity could never create anything or anyone that did not come from Love. Love can only beget Love; it can do nothing else."

"That type of Love is rarely seen in our physical world."

"Any energy less than Love is nothing more than an emotional reaction to what is happening in your created environment. If there is anything or anyone you dislike, then your love is emotional not Divine.

"There is no energy greater than love, love of self, love of child, love of parents, love of country, love of belongings, etc., etc., etc. This love, however, is conditional, it ebbs and flows according to conditions presented to it. It is a judgment! Only unconditional Love is free of judgment! If you love something, but not something else, your love is conditional, a judgment."

"I never looked at love as a judgment, Teacher. I thought that the love we know here was a kind of building block towards the all encompassing Love of the Divine."

"When you are able to look with kindness and reverence on all things and people around you without prejudice, then your conditional love is no longer; it has been replaced by the unconditional Love of the Divine. If you want to be loved, you must first love others. We are loved to the degree we love others. Here is a quote from Ralph Waldo Trine:

> 'This is the Spirit of Infinite Love. The moment we recognize ourselves as one with it we become so filled with love that we see only the good in all. And when we realize that we are all one with this Infinite Spirit, then we realize that in a  sense we are all one with each other. When we come into a recognition of this fact, we can do no harm to any one, to any thing...Love grows and reigns supreme Then, wherever we go, whenever we come in contact with the fellow man, we are able to recognize the God within.'

"Love is, perhaps, to most, and quite possibly, the least understood energy of all the pillars. Divine Love, the highest level, is unconditional. It does not rely on conditions or circumstances like human love does. Divine Love flows freely without seeking anything in return; it is infinite and unchanging, encompassing everything and everyone without exception."

"Am I to understand that Divine Love can only exist in Divine Truth and, furthermore, can only be expressed therein?"

"Yes Hans, Divine Love can only exist within Divine Truth! For it is here, in the Oneness, where Love can truly be expressed and experienced. It is here where it evaporates the illusion of separation, embracing us in the arms of a universally connected Divinity. One cannot achieve Divine Truth without embracing Divine Love for Love is the energy within which the Divine has its *Being*."

***********

And just like that my conversation with Teacher came to an end and I found myself in the peaceful garden where Malachi usually made his presence known. He arrived quickly and before I could utter a greeting, he delved right into the continuation of Love.

"Hans, at the human level, however, love is seen as an emotion, underlying the highs and lows of daily living. It ranges from the parental affection for a child to the passionate expression culminating the affection between a man and woman. These acts of Love are not separate from Divine Love; they are its reflection through the human experience. Since humans are not aware of their Truth, the height of their Love experience is equally limited."

"How is that so, Malachi?"

"Trapped in the illusion of separation, the ego resists the unifying nature of Love by attempting to protect its own power. In order to move beyond the ego into the consciousness of Love one must embrace the realm of silence, humility, and simplicity. For it is here that our hearts become open and accepting of others. It is within these parameters that meditation and internal prayer become contemplative to the point where Love truly becomes an expression of the Divine.

"Love," Malchi continued, "is probably the most misconstrued and misunderstood word in your society. It's being used as a noun, as a verb and even somehow portrayed as an adjective. If you were to ask ten people what their definition of love is, you may receive ten different answers; love is a feeling, love is a description, love is an action. Most of the time, however, we use the word love to describe our feelings for another person. It was Anonymous who probably described love in the best and most meaningful way possible:

> 'Love is patient, love is kind. It does not envy, it does not boast, it is not proud. It is not rude, it is not self-seeking, it is not easily angered, it keeps no record of wrongs. Love does not delight in evil but rejoices with the truth. It always protects, always trusts, always hopes, always perseveres.'

"Yet love is that universal embodiment of everything that is good, everything that is right with the world. 'Love conquers all,' as the saying goes, is the undeniable champion of all emotions and feelings. Through love you enter a dimension where evil, fear or any other transgressions are overcome; you enter a world of peace, joy and empathy. As Gandhi stated so aptly, 'Where there is love there is life.'"

"The way I understand it, love is anything one likes, anything encompassing goodness and those giddy, emotional feeling filling our bodies while clouding our judgment when a special someone arrives. Love, quite simply, defines everything good in this world and in our lives. But it is, most often, associated with feeling and, therefore, is primarily defined as a sensation or emotion acting on us in a positive and endearing way. Love is the deepest and most vulnerable emotion known to man."

"Right you are Hans, but while this feeling of love can reach euphoric heights in the individual, it can never describe the love associated with God. Love, in the realm of the Divine can never be a feeling or an emotion rising and falling according to the situation or relationship. Within God, Love is an existence; it never varies and never falters. God is a state of Love impossible to replicate in our lives, but God is more: God is Love!

"Your big dichotomy: is love a feeling or an existence? Feelings diminish over time while Love's existence is eternal. Death itself is not an end to all things, it's simply a transition from our physical state to the spiritual state of Love. Another quote from Trine:

> 'Tell me how much one loves and I will tell you how much they have seen God. Tell me how much they love and I will tell you how much they live with God. Tell me how much they love and I will tell you how far into the Kingdom of Heaven - the kingdom of harmony - they have entered, for 'love is the fulfilling of the law.'

'There are loyal hearts, there are spirits brave,
There are souls that are pure and true,
Then give to the world the best you have,
And the best will come back to you.
Give love, and love to your heart will flow,
A strength in your utmost need,
Have faith, and a score of hearts will show,
Their faith in your word and deed.'"

"Let me describe to you the Five Pillars of Love, Hans."

"What are they, Malachi?"

"The first pillar is Unconditional Love. It simply implies Love without conditions or attachments. It further recognizes that everyone and everything is a reflection of Divine Oneness experiencing itself through Love.

"The second pillar acknowledges compassion, which is, quite simply, Love in action. Here one understands that each person is seeking happiness just like we are. Through compassion we turn enemies into friends.

"The third pillar is unity, understanding we are all connected through Divine Oneness. Here all barriers are removed between the self and others. When fully understood and embraced, unity opens the door to enlightenment.

"The next pillar is service. Service is Love in motion. One cannot embrace Spiritual Love and sit idly by; Love compels action, expecting nothing in return. While Mother Theresa is a great example of a person dedicated to service, one does so through the simple acts of listening, kindness, and teaching.

"And the final pillar is wisdom, which ensures Love is not blind or enabling. Wisdom allows one to set boundaries while reminding us that love must be embraced within as well as without. Wisdom helps one to balance Love and Truth, becoming a transformative force in the process."

"Am I correct in assuming that the great masters, like Jesus and

Buddha, lived theses principles thereby radiating Love to everyone and everything? And that we are all capable of embodying these Pillars of Love?"

"Yes Hans! Awaken the Love within you and realize your Divine Nature!"

# Chapter 7

## The Four Pillars of Divinity: Peace

*"Peace is to be found only within, and unless one find it there they will never find it at all. Peace lies not in the external world. It lies within one's own soul."*

Ralph Waldo Trine

"Among the Four Divine Pillars, Peace stands as the still center, the equilibrium from which all growth and spiritual clarity emerge. It is both a state of being and a dynamic force that guides us toward wholeness. To embrace the Pillar of Peace is to recognize that true tranquility arises not from the absence of conflict but from the presence of harmony within oneself and with the world."

"Teacher, what exactly is the Pillar of Peace all about?"

"Peace, my dear Hans, is, at its core, the recognition of the Oneness of all things. Peace is the stillness residing within, bringing a divine balance to all things. While it may appear to be a passive state, as the Buddha knew in his quietness, it is actually an active engagement with the day-to-day challenges that present themselves. In addition, Peace provides the internal clarity and insight necessary for the creative process."

"How does that happen?"

"Within the peaceful mind exists the Truth of all there is, without distortion. Here Peace is seen as the foundation for embracing the Divine."

"How is this Peace achieved?"

"It begins with self awareness, as do all of the Pillars. To realize Peace one must first overcome the internal turbulence created by fear, emotions, and attachments. An honest self-assessment addressing all unresolved issues, that lie deep within the confines of our psyche, must be taken. Once acknowledged and remedied, one can enter each moment without judgment, while releasing the internal struggle that creates conflict."

"How does this help, Teacher?"

"By accepting each moment as it is, and understanding its Divine connection, one can easily embrace forgiveness, which keeps anger and resentment in check and not allow them to disturb the calmness and understanding within. Most importantly, once you align with Peace you become agents of unity by contributing to the well-being and unity of the entire planet. A true bond of Brotherhood is the result. As the *Urantia Book* states, 'One cannot proclaim the Fatherhood of God while ignoring the brotherhood of man.'"

"It seems to me that humility, simplicity and silence are the primary tools of Peace, Teacher."

"They certainly are, but they are just as important when you're searching for Truth, Love and Joy. Remember, the Four Pillars are designed to liberate you from the throes of fear and attachment, while delivering you to the Oneness within. It is only by your acceptance of these Pillars that you can truly know who you are. These Pillars are not separate from one another, but they are intricately embedded with one another that to know one is to know them all."

"Peace is to be found only within, and unless one find it there they will never find it at all. Peace lies not in the external world. It lies within one's own soul" (Trine)

"So we're not talking about peace that exists between men or nations?"

"No Hans. I'm talking about an inner mindfulness that exists within as you focus on the moment of Now. Here you can observe in the stillness what is happening around you. Here we can observe without becoming engaged, allowing us to respond calmly and with clarity. In doing so you minimize the effects of the ego, its attempt to continually sew the seeds of separation and conflict. This requires a sense of unity within the Oneness, for only there can you recognize that the wellbeing of others affects you as well.

"Fear is another obstacle that Peace must overcome. It continually raises its specter through your internal vulnerability and unassuredness that exists in your world of separation. This becomes a recurring theme until the security of Truth, Love, and Peace have become your identity, have become the foundational awareness of who you really are."

"If I'm to understand this correctly Teacher, at the heart of Peace lies the tranquility, balance, and harmony we seek in every aspect of our lives. This, then, becomes an ongoing practice to stay within and align with the soul in what Walter Starcke calls 'The Third Appearance,' where the physical and spiritual self are engaged in perfect alignment, with a common purpose and direction. For only when the physical self and Spiritual Self are in alignment can the soul be freed to fully express itself."

"It appears that daily Spiritual practices, such as prayer, are needed to keep one from digressing off the path to Oneness."

"Hans, once you are on the path to Oneness, your life becomes a living prayer because you are in constant contact with your Divine Self. Your Divine Self becomes the guiding Light through which Peace makes itself known."

************

"Peace is a state of being! It is not an agreement between people to treat each other civilly. It is an inner calmness and acceptance, which understands what is happening around you, cannot harm you. Peace brings an inner clarity, which recognizes all things are Spiritual. That recognition causes Love to flow inward and outward while creating an acceptance of all that is happening around you, whether good or bad.

Through Love one recognizes only the good within others, regardless if they themselves don't see it."

"So Love and Peace are integrally connected, Malachi?"

"Yes Hans. With the acceptance of Peace one can only respond to events with Love, unconditional Love and that type of Love only exist once you have found your Truth. Truth can only exist in the I Am, Love can only exist where Truth is recognized and Peace can only exist where Love is embraced."

"I'm beginning to see the correlation Malachi. Divine connection can only be recognized by *Being*, and thereby all the energies of divinity flow easily in, around, and through us."

"Yes. Peace fosters an acceptance of all people and things for Peace recognizes the Oneness of all there is. If you are not peaceful to another, you are not peaceful within yourself."

"So Peace, much like Love, starts with the self."

"Exactly. Within the presence of Peace there are no prejudices or fighting, within Peace lie only brotherhood, acceptance, and empathy. The peaceful hand reaches out to anyone, regardless of one's beliefs or distrust. Peace has no enemies, Peace never seeks retribution, Peace always lends a helping hand. Within the omnipotence, omniscience, and omnipresence lie Truth, Love, and Peace. One cannot exist without the other."

"So if I'm correct, Malachi, Peace does not tolerate, it accepts; Peace does not judge, it accepts; Peace does not bargain, it accepts. Peace, like Love, is unconditional."

"That about sums it up, Hans. If I might add a quote by Ralph Waldo Trine: 'Peace is to be found only within, and unless one find it there they will never find it at all. Peace lies not in the external world. It lies within one's own soul' And, to be more precise, 'To be at one with God is to be at peace.'"

"What about fear? Doesn't fear affect one's acceptance of Peace, Malachi?"

"Again I'll quote Ralph Waldo Trine:

'The moment we fear anything we open the door for the entrance of the actualization of the very thing we fear... When we come into harmony with the   Spirit of Peace, evil reports and apparent bad treatment, either at the hands of friends or of enemies, will no longer disturb us. When we are conscious of the  fact that in our life and our work we are true to that eternal principle of right, of truth, of justice that runs through all the universe, that unites and governs all, that always eventually prevails, then nothing of this kind can come nigh us, and come what may we will always be tranquil and undisturbed'

"Fear is for the weak at heart, for the ones who lack the mindfulness of the Divine. Hans, fear can only exist where Truth, Love, and Peace do not."

"The furtherance of evolution depends upon our ability to sense a unity with nature and her forces. When the knowledge of this unity comes alike to all people, the tread of armies will cease and the bugle call will echo the soft notes of brotherly love. In mental and spiritual healing, the supremely important thing to emphasize is the presence of good and its perfect unity with the individual."

(Holmes, *Can We Talk to God*)

"Malachi, does Peace have its own internal pillars like Love does?"
"Yes, You can say that."
"What might they be?"
"The First Pillar of Peace is acceptance, the ability to accept your reality as it is without resistance."
"Is this the same as surrender Malachi?"
"Yes Hans, surrender simply accepts life as it, living in harmony with its natural flow. You might have heard the Serenity Prayer?"
"God, grant me the serenity to accept the things I cannot change,

the courage to change the things I can, and the wisdom to know the difference."

"Very good Hans. Using the Serenity Prayer as a starting point, we free ourselves to work with life rather than against it.

"The second pillar is detachment. This is critical as Spiritual Peace is impossible when we are attached to people or possessions. Detachment recognizes that nothing in this world is permanent. It trusts whatever enters your space is part of a greater Divine Order, including loving without possessions, supporting without expectations, and embracing life with grace."

"It seems like letting go is at the heart of everything."

"If you truly seek enlightenment during your lifetime, letting go is paramount, Hans."

"What is the next pillar, Malachi?"

"Presence or living in the Now. Peace is only found in the present moment. As the Buddha said, 'Do not dwell in the past, do not dream of the future, concentrate the mind on the present moment.' By practicing the presence one quiets the mind of endless chatter, while experiencing life as it enters your space. Here we discover that Peace is something we realize moment to moment, not something we need to seek."

"Isn't that true of all the pillars, Truth, Love, Peace, and Joy can only be realized in the present moment?"

"Yes Hans. The Now is the only place where anything happens at all, regardless of what it is.

"The Fourth Pillar of Peace is trust. It is trust that allows us to let go of fear, doubt, and anxiety. Through trust we allow life to unfold before us knowing that even challenges serve a higher purpose. You might see faith, the realization there is a higher power, wisdom, beyond our understanding, as important here."

"Over time faith becomes a knowing, does it not Malachi?"

"Over time faith becomes a knowing and trust becomes second nature. Peace follows naturally, Hans."

"I understand."

"The last is alignment, which simply acknowledges one to live in accordance to Divine Principles. As one aligns his or her thoughts, words, and actions with Truth, Love, and Integrity, profound Peace will be realized."

"Do good, be good, and think good in everything you say and do, without exceptions."

"That is correct Hans. Alignment means to speak honestly, embracing Love while letting go of fear, and living with a sense of purpose. Through alignment one becomes a conduit of peace for him or herself as well as others.

"These Five Pillars of Peace, acceptance, detachment, presence, trust and alignment create the solid foundation for spiritual Peace. This is an internal Peace, not one dependent on external circumstance. It allows one to walk through his or her daily world with calm and confidence."

"Yea, though I walk through the valley of the shadow of death, I will fear no evil: for thou art with me; thy rod and thy staff they comfort me." (Psalm 23:4)

"Yes Hans, that is your Peace."

# Chapter 8

## The Four Pillars of Divinity - Joy

*" Joy is the realization of the truth of one-ness, the oneness of our soul with the supreme love."*

Rabindranath Tagore

*" I accept my privilege, as Its expression, of manifesting the Life, Love, Peace, Strength, Harmony, and Joy of God - the Almighty Presence who dwells within me and incarnates in me, as me."*

Ernest Holmes

Divine Joy is the euphoric energy, which only enlightenment can give. It is the joining of one's internal and external self, creating a unified sense of one's true self which, Walter Starcke calls the "Third Appearance." Divine Joy frees the soul to be all it can be, allowing it to celebrate life fully. With Truth, Love, and Peace as its bedrock, Joy rises to its unconditional Self.

Joy dissolves fear, judgment, and despair replacing them with hope, gratitude, and forgiveness, thereby aligning the soul with its Divine purpose of spreading Love and Peace to all corners of the universe. Joy is capable of raising its vibration to align itself with the Divine Oneness. Joy tosses aside past memories and future desires by forever remaining in its meaningful moment of Now. Within Joy exists that internal guiding Light fueling an internal bliss, which is Divinely connected.

This self-sustaining pillar is present within the confines of unconditional Love and Peace. It is an energy that is continually returned as well as given. Within this cycle lies a pure heart and an unconditional acceptance of all there is. Recognizing everything as a creation of the Divine, Joy doesn't just recognize its surrounding beauty and grace, but it is an integral part enhancing every moment by opening itself up to the Divine creative flow.

Joy is not something one creates or receives by doing good deeds, but it is an outgrowth of the Love and Peace that exists within. Connecting with the Divine erases the self-serving needs of the ego while creating a never-ending connection with the eternal Self.

As Love and Peace free the soul to all it can be, Joy becomes its natural expression. Through this expression we celebrate all our creations knowing that the Divine is co-creating with us.

"Within Joy exist gratitude, connection, purpose, playfulness, and love," Malachi explained.

"Please explain."

"Gratitude erases negativity within one's life."

"How so, Malachi?"

"It is gratitude that allows you to see the beauty and abundance around you, without judgment. Through gratitude a shift from lack to abundance occurs and a shift from wrong to right. It was the Apostle Paul who stated, 'Rejoice always, pray continually, give thanks in all circumstances (1 Thess. 5:16-18),' and Buddhism teaches us to be grateful for each moment, for each moment is a gift unto itself."

"Malachi, does gratitude only exist in the Now?"

"When you think about it, it makes sense. How can you be grateful for something that hasn't occurred yet? By the same token, how can you be grateful for something that has passed you by? Sure you can relive the laughter and realize its positive impact, but by delaying your gratitude you've missed the true meaning behind the experience. You can relive, but never repeat."

"Because every experience is an occurrence unto itself."

"Very good Hans. Focus on gratitude and greater things will enter your life."

"So gratitude is not about 'thank you' but rather about being immersed in the experience, embracing that which is happening at the present moment."

"Yes Hans, when we extend gratitude to our experiences, it slowly becomes a way of life, and joy is sure to follow."

"What is connection about, Malachi?"

"Connection is a basic spiritual principle mired in Truth, Hans. It's a connection with the Divine, with others, and with the natural world around us."

"Are you referring to the Oneness?"

"Of course! Once you realize that we are all connected your experiences will heighten a hundred fold. You will no longer feel isolated but you will experience boundless belonging, an integral connection to all things. What could bring greater Joy than that?"

"Can you explain that a little more? I'm not quite sure how that can happen."

"Connect with the Divine through faith, meditation and purpose. Aligning with the Universe will bring happiness and Peace into your life, overcoming all worldly concerns.

"Connecting with others builds friendships as experiences are shared, deepening a sense of Joy while expanding the soul connection between individuals. And connecting with nature enhances your sense of wonder and awe. Walk in the forest or watch the ocean waves or just feel the warmth of the sun and you will know what I mean."

"Yes Malachi, I have enjoyed many such days where peace and quiet embrace the entire body creating a sense of humility, silence, and simplicity. It makes one realize that the joy gained through the hustle and bustle of the material world is short lived."

"Correct Hans. Joy is not something belonging to the individual, but it's a universal emotion meant to be shared, and the more you share it, the greater the Joy will be."

"It fills the soul!"

***********

Without realizing how it happened, I suddenly found myself on Teacher's white, marble bench.

"How did I get here?"

"Your connection to Joy brought you here."

"How?"

"Your desire to learn more about Joy. Desire is a high level of vibration, which connects you with similar levels of vibrations. The filling of your soul brought you here."

"Will you complete this lesson then?"

"Yes. I believe purpose, or the fulfillment of the soul is the next topic. Purpose is the soul's calling, the reason you are born to the physical world. Purpose doesn't need to be earth shattering, it's just something that needs to be meaningful to you."

"Like writing this book."

"Yes, like writing this book."

"How does that happen, Teacher?"

"By aligning our sense of value and creative gifts, we experience Joy at a much higher level. Everyone is an artist with special gifts, painters, writers, teachers, healers, adventurers, athletes, etc. Joy is not realized by sitting idly by waiting for inspirations to emerge, rather it is realized by doing! As Picasso so aptly stated, 'The meaning of life is to find your gift. Your purpose is to give it away.'

"To nurture purpose one must allow one's internal soul energy to flow outward freely. Listen to your inner calling and your Joy will set you free, your life will become electric as the energy of purpose melds your physical and spiritual selves into Walter Starcke's Third Appearance. What greater Joy could there be?"

"Wow, I can feel the energy, Teacher."

"As you should. You're experiencing Joy in action!

"Let's continue with playfulness. As Jesus said, 'Unless you become like little children, you will never enter the kingdom of heaven" (Matthew 18:3). For some reason religion and spirituality are looked at solemnly, taking the joy out of the experience. True spirituality elevates one's internal grasp of life to a whole new joyful level.

"The soul does not sit silently by as one follows the path to enlightenment; the soul yells out loud, with all its euphoric splendor, spreading the joyful news near and far. Spiritual growth and awakening is not a solemn endeavor, it's pure Joy. Here the soul can bask in the experience and become what it was intended to be: Pure Joy."

"So we can laugh as we climb the ladder of consciousness to be who we really are?'

"Not only can you laugh and be lighthearted, it's a requirement! Let me repeat that: It's a requirement to laugh and be lighthearted if you follow the road to enlightenment. Is that not what Joy is?

"Is Joy not contained within the energy of Love? Is Love not the energy of the Divine? To love and to be loved is the purest form of Joy imaginable.

"While Love is a pillar unto itself, Love is what makes Joy possible. Joy is impossible without Love."

"That certainly makes sense to me, Teacher."

"As it should. Let me also tell you that Love creates Joy in several ways. First is self-love, which creates inner Joy by informing you that you are already enough. You don't have to prove anything to anyone. Next is Love for others, which expands Joy by embracing your neighbor and receiving it back in return. And finally there's the Love for the Divine. Here the deepest form of Joy is realized as you're connected to the everlasting Source of Love itself."

"By embracing gratitude, connection, purpose, playfulness, and love we will know true Joy. This Joy is not something I strive for, but it already exists within me, waiting to be awakened. By including these aspects into my life I will not experience joy, I will become Joy. This reminds me of awakening to who we really are."

"It should Hans. For all you really are, is already inside you. *Becoming* all you really are is not a journey. It's not an arduous trek through life requiring you to do anything. It's simply surrendering to your soul's desire to awaken the Divinity within you. You are a creation of the Divine, as such you are an expression of the Divine. Your *Being* was birthed from Divine Being; therefore you can be nothing less. So go, and be who you really are!"

# Chapter 9

## Choosing Your Path

*"The consciousness of separation, segregation, superiority - of 'we' versus 'they,' of 'us' and 'them' - is what creates the Hitler Experience. The consciousness of Divine Brotherhood, of unity, of Oneness, of 'ours' rather than 'yours/mine' is what creates the Christ Experience."*
Neale Donald Walsch

"As you continue to enhance your belief system Hans, let's take a brief look at what is not required and what should not be part of that belief."

"I agree Malachi. It's always good to know what is required or expected of you, but that can, at times, become counter productive. Knowing what is not included helps to strengthen one's internal resolve and help in determining what should be included."

"Then let me begin with the behavioral umbrella called sin, which continually makes its presence known from most pulpits. You wrote a poem a while ago that seems appropriate here. It's called "Whispers in the Street," remember?

"Yes I do."

"Here it is:

'They say they know what's best for me,
As we gather one and all.
They understand what's right and wrong for me,

"

# HANS BENES

Summer, winter, spring and fall.
They understand my every purpose,
They're caring and so sweet,
Life's evolving as predicted by,
Those whispers in the street.

Those whispers, although silent
Shout a language all their own,
Passing from one another
Hearsay, which has been sown,
Changing lives which are so fragile,
Reaping harvests still unknown.

But why should I persist and listen,
To experts self-proclaimed?
Who know and predict the future,
As if it were prearranged.
But who gives these whispers their substance,
Determines their valid state?
It's a code, which has not been written
Yet determines people's fate.

Whispers which breed a generation,
Sending it on its way,
Whispers which create a dogma, but
Have nothing valid to say.
Yes, we've created an entire nation
Of citizens so discreet,
While marching to the beating drum,
Of whispers in the street.

Whispers shouting boldly,
Demanding to be heard!
Giving substance to all rumors

Including those unheard
Whispers, which control behavior
Of lives as yet unfurled.

Can anyone stand up and resist
Those whispers in the street?
Do you posses the strength and courage
To stand on your own two feet?
Do you dare to change and be different and
Oppose pretenders of the beat?
And rid this place of vicious lies,
Those whispers in the street?

The truth, it lies hidden
Beneath the will of man
Embracing love and kindness
Since the moment of time began
Its voice is heard in whispers
Like sonatas by Chopin
Embracing that voice of intuition
Within the hearts of man!'

"You address very important subject matters here, directives established by society, which, more importantly deepen the idea of separation. It is a continuous struggle, which has, and continues to create, a society predicated on separation. Dualism, the separation of man and God, is still a cornerstone of humanity's belief system. Let me explain.

"You have all grown up in a world filled with dos and don'ts, rights and wrongs and good and evil. These values have been ingrained in your society for eons and they continue to drive behavior today and for the foreseeable future. These beliefs have driven the human condition to unimaginable heights and accomplishments. Doing what's right often leads to societal rewards and acknowledgment while the opposite normally leads to chastisement and exclusion.

"Modern society has built a whole system of law and order regarding these values. As Thomas Paine once said, 'It is the duty of every man, as far as his ability extends, to detect and expose delusion and error.' Law and order not only dictate a system of individualistic rights but they also provide a structure for personal behavior. Paine goes on to say, 'Some people can be reasoned into sense, and others must be shocked into it.'

"Religion recognizes these civil laws, but further defines acts of non-compliance to the divine order as sin. Sins are not only a deviation from the civil rules of law and order, but also breaking the expectancies of a higher order, God. Sin, therefore, is not only a physical transgression against the state, but it includes ungodly, mental thoughts as well. Not only is one expected to act according to societal norms, but one is also expected to think a certain way. A system of penance has been adopted by religions that, in many cases, supersede the laws enacted by government. Civil law can only dictate and enforce acts affecting man during his lifetime; religious decrees go beyond that through the declaration of otherworldly punishment in the fires of hell.

"Both secular and spiritual decrees are predicated on a system of severity. Murder, for example, is more serious than stealing. While both warrant punishment, that punishment, however, is predicated on the seriousness of the infraction. Inherent in both systems is an expectancy of behavior often determined by civil laws and religious commandments.

"These rules of expected behaviors often dominate our actions and formulate our behavioral patterns. Unfortunately, they miss the most important aspect of who we really are. We are inherently expressions of God. We are a part of the universal whole. We are one with God. Therefore, your greatest misdeed can never be a breaking of civil or religious rules or decrees; your greatest sin can never be the failure of seeking forgiveness.

"Your greatest sin is not against the state or religion; your greatest sin is committed against your very selves! Your greatest sin is forgetting who you really are! Your greatest sin is not remembering to look within to reconnect with that Divine Spirit who expresses itself through you! Once you reconnect with your God center, that mustard seed, or Christ Center, that resides within, you will no longer require civil directives or religious decrees to formulate your behavior or actions. Once you realize that within you resides the consciousness required to live your lives in peace and harmony, you will forever reside in a state of bliss. As Thomas Paine also stated, 'The mind once enlightened cannot again become dark.'

"Everyone is on a journey, a journey of fulfillment and meaning; you are on a journey of self-discovery to realize who you really are. Since birth, man has been taught the ways of the world; man has been taught the expectancies of your society; man has been taught the meaning of relationships; you have been taught to express yourselves freely; and you have been taught the existence of a higher power. These teachings, while certainly valuable and meaningful, have, however, separated you from the underlying truth of who you really are.

"The ways of the world have listed numerous rules and guidelines for you to live by. Many of these guidelines have led you into directions that only serve to separate you further from the truth. Is it any wonder that many of you search for purpose and happiness throughout your lifetime? Happiness and purpose do not lie far away in some distant land; they do not lie hidden on some mountaintop or beneath the vast ocean. Happiness is within the reach for everyone. And once you find that happiness, your purpose will become abundantly clear: spread your secret of happiness throughout the world, to every man, woman and child. This is the "good news" Jesus proclaimed so frequently and passionately.

"The Bible states, 'So God created man in His own image; in the image of God He created him; male and female He created them (Genesis 1:27).' God is Love! 'For God created man to be immortal, made him to be an image of his own eternity (Solomon 2:23).' God is Love! Once mankind comes to realize that everyone is made in the image of God then, people must also realize that they are made in the image of Love. Love is never a state of mind; Love is a state of *Being*. Upon re-awakening to the state of Love, all mankind will come to realize that all of man's temporal laws and all of the religious dogma permeating this world today are unnecessary, for Love trumps them all. 'Anyone who does not love does not know God, because God is love (John 4:8).'

> 'Let the morning bring me word
> of your unfailing love,
> for I have put my trust in you. ...
> God is love.
> Whoever lives in love
> lives in God,
> and God in them' (Psalm 143:8)

"'In my Father's house are many mansions: if it were not so, I would have told you. I go to prepare a place for you. (John 14:2).' You are all mansions within Divine Spirit! 'Do you not know that you are God's temple and that God's Spirit dwells in you (1 Corinthians 3:16)?' You only need to awaken to the truth: God is within you, just as you are within God. It cannot be any other way; otherwise God's omnipresence would have no meaning. Without omnipresence God would not be infinite; and without being infinite God could not be eternal. It, therefore, stands to reason that as God is, so are we!

"Your sole purpose in life, therefore, is to awaken to who you really are. That quest escapes the vast majority of God's children who seek purpose and solace in their material existence. True happiness can never be found where it doesn't exist! True happiness is never realized through friends, possessions or beliefs; true happiness can only be found in the loving grace of the Divine. That happiness is not scattered through the four corners of the world, that happiness lies deep within the Self.

"There's another poem, which simplifies and encapsulates all I have just told you. It's called, 'I Search:'

> "I search,
> Not for justice or joy,
> For they are within my reach.
> I search,
> Not for richness and wealth,
> For they are within my reach.
> I search,
> For peace and harmony
> And brotherhood and love.
> I search,
> For truth and bliss,
> As it exists in the Divine.
> I search,
> For all that I need,
> Through that eternal passageway,
> That lies within."

"Let me conclude this little lesson by stating that a fervent belief of Divine Oneness is required if one is to follow their true spiritual path. One's true spiritual path lies deep within the Self and to reach it one must have a firm grasp of what and where Divine Spirit resides. The answer is, of course, within; Divine Spirit never exists in a state of separation. So, the first basic belief one must embrace is the principle of Oneness. One cannot know God or themselves without understanding everything belongs to the Cosmic Whole, God exists in everyone and everything just as everyone and everything exists within God.

"The second principle that will carry you along the spiritual path is the knowing that God is Love and God loves unconditionally. This unconditional love includes everyone and everything, in spite of what any individual may proclaim. God loves the Hitlers as much as the Mother Theresas. Jesus loved Jew and Gentile alike; he had no favorites and preached his simple Gospel of love and acceptance to anyone who would listen."

"Does that include the old saying of loving your neighbor as yourself?" I interrupted.

"Yes," Malachi continued. "All other spiritual principles originate within these two concepts of Oneness and Love. Within Oneness you will find brotherhood and equality and freedom and non-judgment. Within Love you will find forgiveness and empathy and philanthropy and an internal moral compass, which supersedes all the rules and regulations society has created. 'All You Need Is Love' by John Lennon and Paul McCartney encapsulates this simple principle by stating, 'Love is all there is.' Once you fully understand and embrace this Truth, you will have completed your *Believing* process and are ready to begin *Becoming*."

"Becoming what, Malachi?"

"Becoming what you believe. One cannot claim to believe in a principle without living and acknowledging that principle in their daily lives. To say you believe and not live your belief is professing a lie."

"For what has a man achieved when all the knowledge he possesses has not been manifest in his experience?" I interjected.

"Exactly! One can easily talk the talk, but it becomes more difficult to walk the talk. And until one walks their talk, their internal value system has not been fully formalized. It's easy to claim love for everyone, but it's quite different to show and live love for everyone. It takes courage to live one's belief, while it is shameful to internalize a belief without demonstrating it to the world."

"Thank you Malachi, I'm beginning to get a more comprehensive meaning of letting go."

"Yes Hans. Teacher has some further insight for you as well. I hope you're beginning to realize that all we're sharing with you is not some deep, unknown secret. Love and bliss have been readily available to you and every other person by simply understanding who you really are."

# BELIEVING BECOMING BEING

**************

The energy was pure and whole. Waiting for Teacher has become one of my favorite activities as it offers me time to enter the silence, a place where all things make sense and there is never turmoil. I began to re-live my life, realizing my whole life has been formulated by expectancies, expectancies from my parents, from my teachers, from my friends, from my social norms, from my family and, as I was told, from my God.

Joy and happiness were temporary states residing within the mental concept of "good." Life, therefore, became a constant search for "good" while attempting to avoid a sense of "bad." Life became centered around a search for material worth, which rolled up and down like a continuous ocean wave.

As I sat within my moment of silence, I felt an increase of the Love energy, which always preceded the arrival of my spiritual guide. This energy surpassed any feelings that would rise within me; it brought trust and truth and joy. I trusted it implicitly!

"Hello Teacher, it's always a delight to meet with you."

"Likewise Hans, it gives me great joy to know you are well along your spiritual path. I would be glad to help you in any way possible."

"Thank you, Teacher. I have been talking with Malachi about embracing a belief system that would help me look within and resurrect a new Hans."

Teacher chuckled, "You have it right Hans, your journey within is, indeed, a resurrection. As you go deeper and deeper, a new Hans will emerge, one who understands and embraces the Oneness of all things. But you won't get there by believing."

"What do you mean Teacher? I thought building a belief system is the pre-requisite to *Becoming*."

"The process begins with believing and ends with knowing. What you believe must be so ingrained within you that doubt no longer exists. Knowing indicates a deep-set conviction that cannot be shaken regardless of what you see going on around you. It requires faith, a whole lot of faith."

"What exactly is faith, Teacher."

"Faith is knowing things are so despite what your outside world is revealing to you. Faith elevates your vibration of believing to a vibration of knowing. As Walter Starcke states in *It's All God*,

> 'Faith isn't something we have; faith is something we do. Faith is an energy. Faith is the power inherent in what we see or perceive. If faith is the substance of things hoped for, then faith becomes our 'seeing' because what we imagine or see manifests outwardly in form...Faith is the seed we plant in consciousness...You have been given an insurance policy, a spiritual law for faith; a law that will   assure you that faith will create your highest good. That law is, 'seek (see) ye first the kingdom of God'...Plant yourself in God. Then you will have gone beyond faith, because you will 'be' faith.'

"Once you become faith you will 'Know' all things. You will come to realize that you are the one who creates and maintains your separation from God, simply by your beliefs. In Living as God, Raymond Stewart states, 'Separation between you and God is as real as you think it is. God involves a change of attitude, not a return. Paradoxically, our effort to move back into God reinforces the illusion of separation.' (Starcke)

"Am I to assume that to overcome the belief in separation, or the process of letting go, is determined by the strength of our faith in the Oneness?"

"That's partially right, Hans. It's not just embracing the Oneness, it's really about knowing who you are. Knowing who you really are is the total purpose of the '*Believing*' process. When you analyze the '*Believing*' process, you'll notice its a simple spiritual progression from basic belief to faith to knowing. Until you know, you can't become spiritual and you certainly cannot be spiritual."

"There seems to be a real dichotomy here, Teacher."

"Yes there is. Tell me about it.

"It seems to me that in order to live my beliefs, I need to let go of my beliefs."

"That is true, Hans. But also realize that once you begin to live your beliefs, they are no longer beliefs; they have become knowing. And knowing is based on a foundation of unshakeable faith, which will never waiver. As you believe, so you will become."

I sat in silence for quite some time after Teacher departed, realizing my personal belief system was missing a major ingredient. How do I develop an undying faith that leads me to a total transformation from self to Self? For whenever I attempt to analyze the instructions from both Teacher and Malachi, more questions arise in my consciousness. I seem to be caught in a constant quagmire of why and how and where and when. What's the secret of stopping further descent into the proverbial rabbit hole?

"The heart," came my subliminal reply.

I stood up smiling realizing everything that I had been taught originated in the mind. The best times I could remember were those when I was held close in my mother's arms with love flowing freely between us. This was also true when I held my children and my wife. To me, love was a feeling during times of extreme joy and happiness. It was dynamic and often short-lived, easily replaced by some interrupting need. It was time to change my understanding, not only of love, but my whole value system as I understood it. It was truly time to let go and let God or, better yet, let go and let Love.

# Chapter 10

## I Believe

*"There is no place where I leave off as the life of one or begin as the life or mind of another, because all is one. I flow through all, in all, as all. I AM also the flow. I AM in musical sounds, yet I AM the sound itself. Of all creation, I AM the essence, the fiber, the fabric, the form, the action, the very mind and the very life."*

Joel Goldsmith

"Hans, we are what we believe. What does your belief system look like?"

I thought for a moment as my many beliefs surfaced, "There's a lot Malachi."

"Then let me hear it."

"I believe in the following, Malachi:

"We are all creations of the one Universal Energy commonly called God. As His/Her omnipresence dictates, there is no separation from that Oneness by anything or anyone. The Almighty is within us as we are within It.

"Any person able to tap into this Being of Energy, will know, not only themselves, but the Eternal Almighty as well. I believe there are no individuals, only expressions of the Divine.

"I believe that Holy Consciousness permeates throughout the universe and is accessible to everyone. The level of accessibility to this Consciousness is equal to the ability of the individual's awareness.

"I believe this Holy Energy is fed and ever expanding through the Power of Love.

"I believe in the unconditional Love of the Almighty.

"I believe the Christ Energy, filled with love, truth and joy, resides deep within the psyche of every living being throughout the universe. It rises up through the heart.

"I believe that forgiveness is a form of judgment and is only necessary for those who believe in their physical reality of separation.

"I believe the Divine has no need to forgive.

"I believe in reciprocity: as you give so shall you receive.

"I believe I am the physical demonstration of Divine Consciousness, which experiences Itself through me.

"I believe all things vibrate.

"I believe I Am, therefore I think.

"I believe that by raising one's level of vibration, one can access higher levels of Consciousness.

"I believe all men and women are equal. The Almighty favors no one.

"I believe richness is determined by what lies in the heart and not by the amount of currency in one's wallet.

"I believe the I Am is destined to resurrect to the I AM Consciousness. That is to say: the physical self will come to know itself as the Spiritual Self.

"I believe death is nothing more than a gateway to Eternal Wonderment. Once one drinks from the Spiritual cup of All That Is, they will never thirst.

"I believe in only two commandments: Love the Father and Love your neighbor. All other commandments, laws and regulations were created to deal with man's imperfections.

"I believe everyone is on a path to Spiritual salvation regardless of his or her current journey. All roads lead to God and, eventually, everyone will find their way Home.

"I believe there is only Light. Darkness only exists in separation.

"I believe in the inherent goodness of all mankind.

"I believe in the power of silence.

"I believe prayer is an act of receiving rather than an act of requesting.

"I believe in nothing while believing in everything.

"I believe good will always triumph over bad.

"I believe in the God Dichotomy: from with-out to with-in is a journey of letting go of our physical anchors and embracing our Spiritual freedom.

"I choose peace, no matter what.

"Dare to dream, then dream to dare.

"I believe the Almighty has given everyone a gift. As Picasso states, 'The meaning of life is to find our gift; the purpose of life is to give it away.'

"I believe in the goodness and kindness of all that exists and this goodness and kindness will eventually permeate this planet, filling it with Light and Love.

"There is no science that can identify God; there is no philosophy that can define God; God cannot be explained, God can only be experienced.

"Love is, Love was and Love always will be!"

"Very good Hans, that is certainly an all inclusive list. Is there any way to consolidate it somewhat?"

"I guess, but I would have to go through it and see what can be excluded or combined, Malachi."

"I don't think you need to exclude or combine anything, Hans. Wouldn't something like, 'I am Love and I live Love' include all the items you listed?"

"Are you saying that if I use 'I am Love and I live Love' as a mantra, it would incorporate all my beliefs into my daily life?"

"Don't use it as a mantra Hans. Believe it! Become it! Be it! And when you can do that, you will live it in every moment of every day. With faith as your bedrock, everything will fall into place for nothing can shake you and nothing can change who you are. Also, don't forget that within the Oneness there's only Love. Consciousness, vibrations, light, energy, God, ethers, etc., etc., etc., they're all the same using different labels. It does not matter what you call it, it only matters that you embrace it. Love is the engine that drives the spiritual train while consciousness, light, vibrations, energy, ethers and belief in God are resulting by-products. Your only job, should you decide to accept it, is to open yourself up and return to who you really are by re-entering into what is already yours, the Oneness."

"And all it takes is for me to change my beliefs."

"Not so Hans. All it takes is for you to awaken to what already is, to who you really are. Don't be like Judas and sell your soul for pieces of gold. Don't be like Peter and deny your Christ. Believing is not a process of learning and accepting, it's a means of returning home, and it's a means of awakening. As Joel Goldsmith so aptly stated in *Living The Infinite Way*:

> 'That which I am seeking, I am. I already am; it already is; it always is. With that understanding came the realization that I could give up seeking; I could give up searching; I could even give up praying. It already is. And now my prayer is no longer asking or affirming. My prayer is the realization, the recognition, of is.'

"So I can't screw this up?"

"You can't. The end has been predetermined for you Hans. You can drag it out, delay it, but you can never screw it up. As long as one embraces the human, physical paradigm, it will be difficult to embrace Universal Oneness; and as long as one fails to recognize Universal Oneness, one will struggle spiritually. Here materialism is of utmost importance as the world of objectivity is seen as a constant obstruction to life and, more importantly, keeps one's spiritual truths buried deep within."

"So, what happens when one approaches levels of higher vibration?"

"One begins to question the purpose of life and begins to look for true happiness. People begin to realize fulfillment isn't all about personal gain or power. Faith begins to emerge, faith in self and others. Faith begins to erode internal mental blocks as the heart begins to emerge. The doorway to All That Is opens and a new you is born. This new you sees life differently and begins to recognize the inherent goodness in all mankind. One begins the process of critical thinking, questioning, analyzing and recognizing that principles, which had been ingrained in us since childhood may not be entirely accurate. As one question leads to another the door to awakening gradually opens.

"Slowly we begin to hear and understand the words of Joel Goldsmith in *Living the Infinite Way*:

> 'There is only one truth, Omnipresence, and that truth has been revealed, not only   for thousands of years before the Master, Christ Jesus, but it was so marvelously revealed by him, that we of the Western world have come to accept it as authority. But even while we accept it as authority in Scripture, we deny it in our own experience...
>
> It is possible to find ourselves in some sort of hell. It may be a hell of sin or disease, of lack or limitations, but we may be assured of this: We are having that experience only because we have accepted a sense of separation from God.'

"How do you remember all these quotes, Malachi?"
"Omniscience."
"You believe in omniscience?"
"I know omniscience! I live within omniscience! I am omniscience! Omniscience is not something you attain or acquire; omniscience is there for you to access at any time along with omnipotence and omnipresence. Remember, God is within you, just as you are within God; there is no separation. You can believe in whatever you want, but know your truth: Everything you experience exists within the Oneness. Once you know you're truth you will no longer have any beliefs for truth is not subject to

speculation or interpretation, within truth lies knowingness! And once you know you will become."

"Become what, Malachi?"

"Who you really are!

"You need to remember that without knowing you cannot become. You heard of the saying, 'What you believe, you create.' Well, there's no doubt within knowing, not a single ounce."

"Why is that?"

"Because knowing is immersed in truth and truth can never deviate. Truth is, it can never be anything else. That's why Truth is the First Pillar of Divinity."

"Sounds like Goldsmith."

"Yes Hans, Joel Goldsmith knew his truth. And now it's time for you to embrace yours. Your first step in *Becoming* is knowing your truth."

"And that truth is?"

"Who you really are!"

"So before I become, Malachi, I need to let go of who I think I am. I need to let go of my perception of dualism, of separation in both the objective and subjective realm. I need to understand me, my brother and my God are all one. I reside in them as they reside within me."

"At the very least, believe as you stated and you may begin your journey of *Becoming*. Every step you take, every breath you make, every thought you create is an exciting and fulfilling step to a new you. Every rise in consciousness is a resurrection of a new you. Every resurrection casts out the old you, who you will never again be. A new Hans will morph just as a butterfly escapes its cocoon. As you become, you will have many resurrections; your heart will become your primary source of creating. You will undergo a greater understanding of oneness, of consciousness, of love; with every deeper understanding you will raise your consciousness, which will deepen your understanding of oneness, which, in turn, will open your heart to love."

"And as I raise my vibration to a higher consciousness, my knowing will increase to a point where I won't ever go back because love will become my main belief, become a way of life."

"Yes Hans, here's a quote from Neville Goddard that supports what you say:

> "One of the first things man must realize is that it is impossible, in dealing with this spiritual law of consciousness, to put new wine into old bottles or new patches on old garments. That is, you cannot take any part of the present consciousness into the new state. For the state sought is complete in itself and needs no patching. Every level of consciousness automatically expresses itself.
>
> "To rise to the level of any state is to automatically become that state in expression. But, in order to rise to the level that you are not now expressing, you must completely drop the consciousness with which you are now identified. Until your present consciousness is dropped you will not be able to rise to another level...This letting go of your present identity is not as difficult as it might appear to be. The invitation of the scriptures, 'To be absent from the body and be present with the Lord,' is not given to a select few; it is a sweeping call to all mankind. The body from which you are invited to escape is your present conception of yourself with all of its limitations, while the Lord with whom you are to be present is your awareness of being."

"But believing is only the beginning."

"How so?"

"Live your talk, walk your talk, pray your talk. Your talk is your truth. Your truth is your ability to love. Your love defines your connection with the Divine. Your connection to the Divine is who you are this present moment."

"It seems like a full circle that goes round and round."

"Not a full circle that goes round and round, but rather an evolving spiral that continues its climb to the Christ Consciousness and beyond."

"I will become Christ-like?"

"You are Christ-like! You just don't know it yet!"

*"Spiritual autonomy is knowing who and what you are - knowing that you are divine being itself, knowing that the essence of you is divinity."*
Adyashanti

# Becoming

*"Within every individual, far, far within - deeply hidden behind the mask of personal selfhood - is that part of him (her) which is in and of God. Actually, it is the God-Self unfolding as individual spiritual being."*

Joel Goldsmith

# Chapter 11

## Here I Stand

*"Look at every path closely and deliberately. Try it as many times as you think necessary. Then ask yourself, and yourself alone...Does this path have a heart? If it does, the path is good. If it doesn't, it is of no use."*

Carlos Castaneda

Today, the tiny parking lot is empty. The Sanctuary Center in Sedalia holds a special place for me, not only is it quietly energizing but it also offers one a place to purposefully raise their spiritual vibration in preparation for prayer or meditation. The numerous benches offer one a place to sit, walk, read, reflect and spiritually renew their energy in various private settings.

Today I am sitting on a bench near the wishing trees reflecting on a streamer I placed there a few years ago in remembrance of my son, Johnny. Although I tied it tightly around a strong, solid branch, it is no longer here as its message of my love for my transitioned son is floating somewhere in the wind. His energy, I realized, is no longer here, having been absorbed by the omnipresence of the Divine. He, I was sure, had finally found a place he could call home. Home, I realized, was not a place or a house but a place of being where love abounds and peace flows through everyone's conscious awareness. Home is a constant evolving state of grace and it brought a smile to my face knowing my son is in the best place he can be. A brief prayer of remembrance crossed my mind:

*"I am grateful that your trying journey in this world is over and that you have found your everlasting place of love and peace; no more suffering and stress. I realize my sadness was based on my own inner turmoil regarding our relationship. I send you all the love I possibly can and I look forward to our reunion in this world or the next. Know that you're forever in my heart and soul. Blessings to you."*

Wiping a lone tear, I walked through the wishing trees one more time to absorb their energy of unconditional love and peace left by numerous well-wishers. Why were they still here but not Johnny's? Could it be that it was a final sign of his transition from a material world filled with conflict and doubt to a world of endless love and joy? I certainly couldn't blame him for that.

Before walking the meandering path through the grounds, I entered the lone building, a private sanctuary offering a place for introspection and inner peace. Books, contributed by visitors, were available for everyone to read. I added mine to the collection and took a seat. Closing my eyes I began to breathe slow and deep, opening my heart to the moment, slowly entering the silence.

I came to realize that whether it's consciously, physically, emotionally or spiritually, change is inevitable. The only constant, as far as we know, is change, with one exception: Unconditional Universal Love. At every conscious moment, at every place, at every time, God is all there is, encompassing every living being. At any time, at any place, every corner of the universe is filled with Love. So are we! Our great ignorance lies in the world we have created for ourselves. We have created, and accept as our reality, a place of separation based on the input of our five senses and the needs to sustain our physical self. But today I am embarking on a new journey, one I am undertaking by myself to find Myself. Neither my history nor my past religious training can block the emerging Self, yearning to express itself.

A heightened energy overtook me as a sense of purpose flushed over my body. Material dependency only serves to further remove me from spiritual independence. It is time to follow my destiny and awaken the real Hans within; it is time to claim my independence from my dear friends Malachi and Teacher. It is time to follow my spiritual path to the deepest chambers of my internal being, knowing it is a journey I am destined to take alone. I opened my eyes and left the sanctuary to walk its path.

I passed by the five Platonic Solids whose faces are all identical, regular polygons meeting at the same three-dimensional angles. The ancient Greeks held four of the patterns representing the four elements of earth (Hexahedron), air (Octahedron), fire (Tetrahedron) and water (Icosahedron), while the fifth, Dodecahedron, symbolized the universe as a whole. They are part of the Sacred Geometry, a term used to describe the belief certain geometric shapes have spiritual or divine significance. Not quite sure of the exact connection of these solids and spirituality, I continued my walk to the medicine wheel.

The Medicine Wheel teaches us that we have four aspects to ourselves: the physical, the mental, the emotional, and the spiritual. Each must be in balance and equally developed in order for us to remain healthy, happy individuals. Common in our Native American culture I could relate to the importance of balance in our lives. All too often I allowed emotional and mental shortcomings to dictate my physical state. Spirituality became lost in a world of religious dogma I neither understood nor embraced. My visit here, I was hoping, would begin my journey of *Becoming* what Malachi and Teacher had talked about.

The path continued past the Pa-Kua formation, which looked very similar to the yin and yang. It, again, reminded me, whether consciously, physically, emotionally or spiritually, that change is inevitable. The journey of *Becoming*, therefore, is not a journey at all. It's not a trek to get from one place to another; it's an awakening, a realization of who I really am. However, before I begin the journey of remembering who I really am, I must become convinced of who I am not. Without *Believing, Becoming* becomes a pipe dream.

Sitting on a nearby bench I began to delve into my past, highlighting events that dramatically affected my physical and spiritual lifestyle. I realized that coming to America in September 1955 was a stroke of genius on my father's part. It took courage to leave all we've ever known and immigrate to the United States. Hawkins defines this stage thusly:

"This (Courage) is the critical level that distinguishes the positive and negative influences of life. At the level of Courage, an attainment of true power occurs; it is also the level of empowerment. This is the zone of exploration, accomplishment  fortitude and determination. At the lower levels, the world is seen as hopeless, sad, frightening, or frustrating; but at the level of Courage, life is seen to be exciting, challenging, and stimulating...Courage implies the willingness to try new  things and deal with the vicissitudes of life."

It wasn't until my early teens that my parents felt the need to introduce me to religion. What prompted this change was a mystery to me, as I was at the age of Confirmation when our family joined Bethany Lutheran Church in Elmhurst, New York. Based on the teachings of Martin Luther, Lutherans believe in a strict interpretation of the Bible, while seeing Jesus as the Savior of all mankind. It was a dogma I embraced until my high school years when religion became too invasive in my day-to-day living, as my teenage hormones overwhelmed the demands and expectancies of an inflexible religious doctrine created hundreds of years ago. My beliefs, however, were not completely dismissed, but remained in my inner sanctum waiting to be resurrected at some future time when my spiritual spark would reignite. While that moment took years to present itself, I was glad to realize it had finally arrived.

The main reason for coming to the Sanctuary, however, was its labyrinth. Nestled between outcrops of trees it provided a natural setting where peace and quiet helped raise one's spiritual vibrations.

Used by a worldwide community, labyrinths help quiet the mind, calm anxiety, maintain balance in life, enhance creativity and encourage meditation, insight, self-reflection and stress reduction. Walking the labyrinth integrates the body, mind and spirit into one unified construct within the Universal Oneness. This is where my process of *Becoming* would begin.

Before entering the labyrinth I sat on a nearby bench and began to pray:

*"Divine Presence Within, as I stand at the threshold of this labyrinth, I come before you with a longing in my heart to deepen my spiritual connection with all life. I recognize that true spirituality is not merely a destination but a journey, and I humbly ask for guidance and support as I embark on this path of self-discovery and soul exploration.*

*Creator of the Universe, Source of all wisdom and love, I open myself to your presence here and now. Help me to quiet my mind and center my spirit, that I may be receptive to the whispers of your divine guidance as I prepare to walk this labyrinth.*

*Grant me the courage to release any preconceived notions or expectations I may hold about this journey. May I approach it with an open heart and a willing spirit, ready to embrace whatever lessons and insights you have in store for me.*

*As I take my first steps into the labyrinth, I surrender myself to the rhythm of its winding paths and intricate turns. With each twist and turn, may I let go of the distractions of the outside world and sink deeper into the stillness of my inner Being.*

*Guide me, Divine Energy, as I navigate the labyrinth of my own soul. Shine your light upon the dark corners of my heart, illuminating the hidden fears and insecurities that hold me back from fully embracing my spiritual potential.*

*Grant me the courage to face these shadows with compassion and forgiveness, knowing that in acknowledging them, I can begin to transcend them.*

*As I journey towards the center of the labyrinth, may I feel the Divine presence growing ever stronger within. Awaken within me a deeper awareness of the divine presence, pulsating in my every breath, in my every heartbeat. Help me to recognize that I am not separate from you, but an integral part of your vast and infinite creation.*

*In the center of the labyrinth, I pause to rest in the embrace of your love. Here, in this sacred space, may I find solace and renewal, as I commune with your presence in quiet contemplation and prayer.*

*As I begin the journey back out of the labyrinth, may I carry with me the blessings of this sacred encounter. May the insights and revelations I have received continue to inspire me on my spiritual path, guiding me towards a deeper understanding of myself, and my connection to you.*

*Thank you, Divine One, for the gift of this labyrinth and for the opportunity to walk it in search of spiritual growth and enlightenment. May its sacred geometry remind me of the inherent beauty and order of your creation, and inspire me to live my life in harmony with your divine will.*

*In the Holy of Holies, I pray. Amen."*

As I began to realize the significance of entering the labyrinth, I began to further quiet my mind. This time I was prepared to listen to the silence. I closed my eyes one more time before approaching the labyrinth, as I centered on my goal of spiritual awakening. A few deep breaths helped me recognize the message from within:

*The time has come my friend*
*For us to embrace,*
*The time has come my friend*

*To forego this sad place.*
*Our journey though brief*
*Will take us afar*
*Past mountains on high*
*Beyond distant stars.*

*Let our journey begin my friend,*
*Examine your heart.*
*Let our journey begin my friend,*
*We won't stay apart.*
*A new world lies ahead*
*With green grass and blue skies,*
*Painted with love and good will*
*Unknown in our lives.*

*Welcome my friend*
*To an existence unknown,*
*Welcome my friend*
*To the seeds you have sown.*
*Where democracy and law*
*Don't exist high above.*
*There are no concepts professed*
*The noumenon is Love.*

It was a call, not from Malachi or Teacher, but from my Inner Self. For years I had ignored, not only its messages, but its very existence. My inner Spirit had risen from the silence to lead me through the process of *Becoming.*

*"Have faith! Have faith, not in the journey you will be taking, but where this journey will take you, where and how it will end."*

It was uplifting to know my Inner Self was aware and supportive of my plans. But there was also a distinct rumble of doubt originating from within as well. *"Why would you give everything up when you have no idea of the outcome? Open your eyes and look around, see the trees and animals; look at the bright sun and feel the wind's gentle breeze. You're putting everything you've worked for at risk, your home, your family, your job and your friends, things you have worked years for. And you're putting it all at risk for what, a new beginning with an unknown future and potentially fractured relationships?"*

I was torn between my Inner Self and my ego. One offered an eternal spiritual existence of Love and Peace and Joy where everything and everyone was connected through a Universal Oneness. The other offered me fame and notoriety, which I could enjoy and feel through my lens of material senses.

*"You know what your material world is like! You don't have a clue what the invisible spiritual world is like. Is it even real?"*

My internal response came quickly, *"You know all these things Hans. You have seen them and embraced them. Letting go will always lead you to a crossroad of what you can see and feel with what you can experience in your heart. You will forever question who you are and what your purpose in life is if you remain attached to your outer illusion."*

*"I am not an illusion! I am not an illusion!"* came an internal cry sounding more like a plea. *"The illusion is that which you cannot see or smell or touch. Your reality is here where your brothers and sisters live, here where your home offers you security, here where society has created a world of law and order for you, here where you are free to become whoever you want to be."*

I could feel the turmoil rise from within; just then, my heart joyously began to recite the 23rd Psalm:

> *The LORD is my shepherd; I shall not want.*
> *He maketh me to lie down in green pastures: he leadeth me beside the still waters.*
> *He restoreth my soul: he leadeth me in the paths of righteousness for his name's sake.*
> *Yea, though I walk through the valley of the shadow of*

*death, I will fear no evil: for thou art with me; thy rod and thy staff they comfort me.*

*Thou preparest a table before me in the presence of mine enemies: thou anointest my head with oil; my cup runneth over.*

*Surely goodness and mercy shall follow me all the days of my life: and I will dwell in the house of the LORD forever.*

I wiped the turmoil from my mind and began to relive the story of Jesus, realizing I would have to go through my own crucifixion before I could resurrect to my Father's House. It was a journey I could only take by myself, a migration where I would have to overcome my internal fears of letting go. The Kingdom, I realized had one condition:

"You give yourself to it completely, that you turn your whole being over to it...What was required was a radical, unqualified decision for God involving the total person, his thoughts and feelings as well as his behavior...The obtaining of the Kingdom, then, requires the letting go of your present mode of  existence...Once we empty ourselves in this way we become filled. Once we lose our life we find it."

(Robert Perry)

*"Have faith! Embrace your faith! Your faith will make you strong!"*
Rising from the bench, I stood up straight, stretching out my limbs while breathing deeply, while erasing the last, lingering vestiges of internal fear. Courage had come to the forefront. Walking the labyrinth was easy; embracing my rebirth was another matter. A new Hans was on the verge of *Becoming*, and that will take courage. Approaching the entrance to the labyrinth, my heart began to pound as my internal joy rose to a crescendo. Finally, I had overcome my ego as one last thought crossed mind:

*Here I stand,*
*On the precipice of greatness...*
*All it takes is a step!*
*I only need to decide whether it be forward or backward.*
*On the precipice of greatness,*
*Yes, here I stand.*

Knowing that to become a Son of God required the demonstration of being Godlike to my family, friends and neighbors; to love unconditionally, to forgive fully and to help those in need without personal reward or acknowledgment; I took the step.

# Chapter 12

# The Cleansing

*"The ego is the symbol of separation, just as the Holy Spirit is the symbol of peace. What you perceive in others you are strengthening in yourself."*

Lynn Cayce

Closing my eyes and taking a step, I entered another world, one where physical laws and customs were meaningless byproducts of spiritual reality. Breathing deeply, I slowed my heart and drifted into a vast sea of nothingness. I could no longer tell if I was walking or floating or levitating within the labyrinth. My first focus was to cleanse the mind of its ego influence, allowing me to enter the silence where my transformation back to my spiritual roots would begin.

My cleansing began with a silent prayer:

*Divine Spirit, in this sacred moment, I humbly come with an open heart and a willing spirit, seeking guidance and grace. I recognize the limitations of my ego, which often blinds me to the beauty and truth of divine presence. Today, I surrender my ego at your feet, asking for your help in cleansing it from my being.*

*Please, help me release the chains of pride, arrogance, and self-importance that bind my soul. Guide me in letting go of the need for validation and recognition, and grant me the wisdom to see beyond the illusions of separation that my ego creates. Teach me to embrace humility and to walk the path of love and compassion.*

*I acknowledge that my ego has often led me astray, causing me to prioritize my desires over the needs of others, to judge and criticize, and to live in fear rather than faith. I ask for your forgiveness for any harm my ego has caused, and I pray for the strength to overcome its grip on my life.*

*Fill me with light, O Divine One, so that I may become a vessel for love and wisdom. Help me to see others and myself through the eyes of compassion, recognizing the divine spark that resides within each soul. Guide me in cultivating gratitude and contentment, knowing that true fulfillment comes from aligning my will with yours.*

*As I embark on this journey of cleansing the ego, I trust in infinite grace to support me every step of the way. Grant me the courage to face my shadow self with honesty and compassion, and the resilience to persevere through the challenges that arise.*

*May this prayer serve as a sacred invocation, inviting divine presence into my life to purify my heart and soul. With deep reverence and gratitude, I offer myself, trusting in the transformative power of Love.*

*Amen.*

I paused momentarily and fell to my knees within the labyrinth. Retrieving my bottle of water, I blessed it, as I realized a new birth lay before me. From within, I came to understand that personal baptism holds profound significance as a sacred ritual symbolizing spiritual rebirth and cleansing. It marks a deeply personal commitment to my faith, signifying a symbolic immersion into the teachings and principles of my belief system. Beyond its ceremonial aspect, baptism serves as a spiritual milestone, representing my inherent desire for purification and renewal, as I embark on a journey of deeper connection with my divine source. This sacred act not only symbolizes the forgiveness of past wrongdoings but also symbolizes the embrace of a new life, guided by faith, love, and spiritual awakening. Ultimately, personal baptism stands as a testament to my dedication to a spiritual path and an intention to live in alignment with my chosen beliefs.

Leaning my head back, I slowly poured the blessed water through my hair and down my back. Instantly, my heart burst into a divine energy of love, joy, and peace, as my personal forgiveness for all things still harboring within was so powerful that I could feel the light and love grow in my heart. I felt the Oneness as my senses of the external world changed from seeing, feeling and smelling to an unseen awareness of universal connectivity of all things within Divine Consciousness.

"After being baptized, Jesus came up immediately from the water; and behold, the heavens were opened, and he saw the Spirit of God descending as a dove and lighting on Him." (Matthew 3:16)

I realized that this personal baptism surpassed a simple physical cleansing; it embodied a holistic approach of purification, encompassing the realms of the physical, mental, and spiritual. At its core, my personal cleansing not only served as a symbolic act of shedding impurities accumulated within myself, but it also paved the way for a renewed sense of clarity and inner harmony. Opening my heart to Spirit, this purification process helped to facilitate a deeper connection with the divine and the universe, enabling me to rise above the confines of ego and materialism.

In addition, I became aware that personal cleansing fostered self-awareness and introspection, encouraging me to confront my innermost thoughts, emotions, and beliefs. By purging myself of these negative energies and attachments, I could develop a heightened sense of mindfulness and presence, laying the groundwork for spiritual growth and enlightenment. This personal cleansing served as a channel for inner transformation, guiding me towards a state of heightened consciousness and enlightenment. Again, I fell to my knees and closed my eyes as my heart was fully opened to receive. A vision crossed the screen of my mind:

I found myself sitting in a garden where a nearby waterfall fed a meandering stream. Numerous scented flowers of various colors, surrounded by lush, green grass, proudly aimed their petals towards a radiant sun. Butterflies and bees were busy pollinating and drinking nectar.

As I was admiring the scene before me, a lone, white figure approached from the distance. Just like Teacher, its calming aura of love and joy arrived well before it did. Without speaking, it embraced me and signaled for me to follow. With that we levitated above the few clouds sitting in the sky, embarking on a journey to an unknown destination.

Finally we came to a stop and a scene opened before me. I recognized my sister and her husband, with whom I had major differences and dislikes. As the scene unfolded, I began to realize the suffering he had gone through during his lifetime. Lacking love during his childhood, he proceeded to grow into an adult who withheld love from those around him. Material wealth was his main driving force just like it was his father's. Life had become a continuous series of getting, however possible. Joy was lost in a world of materialism.

I began to feel sad, realizing that our relationship was an opportunity for me to bring love and joy into his world. But my own ego prevented me from helping someone I was not fond of. I asked for forgiveness for both him and me. My heart felt lighter as the cleansing of this unresolved issue allowed more light to flow within me. Looking back to the scene, I saw light and a feeling of love penetrate my brother-in-law's heart. My simple act of forgiveness not only helped my joy to grow, but his as well.

"Forgiveness is a powerful tool when *Becoming*!" came the message from my guide.

After cleansing my heart of the negative energy I held for my brother-in-law, my guide led me to another experience. This time we stopped to view several short snippets of me during my lifetime.

It was 1964 when I attended the University of Missouri after graduating from high school. Immature and without properly planning, I left the safety of my home for the very first time. During the admission process, I paid for my tuition, room and board and books with checks that bounced a mile high. Studying became an activity put off till tomorrow until, finally, there were no more tomorrows available. Procrastination had become my close friend.

Simple things like getting my yearly car inspection or balancing my checkbook monthly, became chores, which instilled fear of uncertainty and were thusly delayed until the last possible moment. I was all too happy to let my wife handle the bills and money when she offered to do so. Of course that led to deeper financial issues.

I began to realize how procrastination led to an internal insecurity bordering on fear and creating anxiety throughout the family dynamic. Again, I asked for forgiveness realizing that life could have been so much easier if issues were promptly addressed and dealt with. Once again, I saw the light and love increase as my past procrastinating ways changed.

"Forgiveness is a powerful tool when *Becoming*!" came another message from my guide.

The last scene my guide presented to me was my father on his deathbed. He was under Hospice care and bedridden in a nursing home with a morphine drip to control the pain from his prostrate cancer that had spread to his bones. Not a religious or spiritual man, my father, nevertheless, worked hard, always maintaining a "can do" attitude.

But in the few weeks since being placed under Hospice care, his whole demeanor changed. While the family was filled with sadness, my father's outlook was happy and joyful. Apparently, the morphine had placed him in a deep, unconscious state where he was free to travel between the spiritual and physical realms. He knew what lay before him as his heightened consciousness prepared him for his transition. During this time, I was sure he was able to completely let go of his ego and embrace the Oneness.

He was not afraid to die; in fact he welcomed his last breath. While he was leaving behind a body ravaged by strokes and cancer, he eagerly awaited the freedom of his released soul. Only we, his family and friends, saw his impending death; my father saw it as a personal, spiritual resurrection that usurped all earthly experiences. He was going home.

While I did not fully understand at the time what my father was going through, I knew, from this vision, that our true reality was not this material world, but rather a spiritual consciousness accessible from within our own selves. I smiled as my heart was filled with his love. "Do not fear, Love awaits, I await. You will wake from your dream and bask in the Loving Oneness!" was the last message my father sent.

"Awakening, awareness and acceptance are necessary when *Becoming*!" came a third message from my guide.

We continued on as a variety of historical scenes passed us by. There was the Second World War when 45 million souls lost their lives because political strongmen felt a need for power and control. In the end, no one won as suffering and loss affected almost every family around the globe. The destruction of cities and lives only ensured the creation of a more powerful and vigilant military. Truth, trust and peace were cast along the wayside as a new era of powerful weapons and military supremacy was born.

Moving deeper into history, a time of religious zealots presented itself. Strict religious dogma was enforced upon a populace struggling for survival. God ruled supreme and his appointed "church messengers" had the power to enforce their doctrines with full Heavenly approval. Religious wars and personal torture of perceived non-believers became a normal occurrence. Power lay within the confines of the rich while the poor were pawns in a world that made little sense.

Still further back in time I saw Galgotha with its three crosses, surrounded by Roman guards and mourners. The Son of Man was fulfilling his prophesy of being put to death by the very same people he lived to save. His message of love and peace became an infringement to local powers, both to the occupiers and those occupied. Deep-rooted religious dogma would not succumb to newly enlightened spirituality if it meant any relinquishing of power and means. Man's Laws of

Heaven would not be sacrificed to accommodate a few zealots bent on changing hundreds of years of history.

"Sacrifice is a difficult thing to endure as you travel the path to *Becoming*!" came my guide's message.

We continued our journey through time, visiting the Mesozoic Era with its giant reptiles walking the earth. Their enormous size and ferociousness startled me as I asked to quickly move on. Instantly I found my self in space looking down on our planet, while continuing to move deeper and deeper into space, past our solar system, past our galaxy into the deepest remnants of our universe.

And then, without warning it was all gone in an instant, galaxies, stars and planets were no longer visible. "The big bang?" I asked.

"As best as you can understand," came the reply.

I found myself in a deep void of nothingness; it was like a giant womb awaiting the birth of creation. Yet I was perfectly at ease, there was no fear, only a knowing that a new experience, one filled with Truth and Joy and Love, lay before me.

Darkness, there was nothing but darkness as far as the eye could see. It appeared to continue for infinity, while lasting for untold eons before that first, faint light pierced through. Others soon followed, as darkness and light existed side by side. Oneness, I realized, included both dark and light, heaven and hell, all existing side by side within the Eternal Whole.

It was Hawkins' consciousness scale in action, as any level below 250, neutrality, remained mired in a world of fear and doubt. At 250 a faint light appeared out of the darkness, like the birth of something joyful. As the light intensity increased, I could see its sphere of influence become greater and greater. I was sure, in some distant moment of Now, the darkness would be completely overrun by Light and all will, once again, exist within the Divine Oneness, which knows only Love.

> "But the Kingdom (does) have one condition: that you
> give yourself to it completely, that you turn your whole
> being over to it...What (is) required (is) a radical, unqualified

decision for God involving the total person, his thoughts and feelings as well as his behavior...Therefore, our present mode must be relinquished, it must fall away so that we can enter into the new way that Jesus offers...The obtaining of the Kingdom, then, first requires the letting go of our present mode of existence." (Perry)

Personal cleansing I found, transcends mere physical hygiene; it embodies a holistic approach to purification, encompassing the realms of the physical, mental, and spiritual. At its core, personal cleansing serves as a symbolic act of shedding impurities accumulated within oneself, paving the way for a renewed sense of clarity and inner harmony. I could feel how this purification process facilitated a deeper connection with the divine and the universe, enabling me to rise above the confines of ego and materialism.

In addition, this personal cleansing fostered a self-awareness and introspection, encouraging me to confront my innermost thoughts, emotions, and beliefs. By purging myself of negative energies and attachments, I was able to cultivate a heightened sense of mindfulness and presence, laying the groundwork for spiritual growth and enlightenment. In essence, my personal cleansing served as a catalyst for inner transformation, guiding me towards a state of heightened consciousness.

I began to realize, practices such as fasting, meditation, and prayer are integral components of personal cleansing and would further my spiritual ascendance. Fasting, for instance, purifies the body and mind, promoting self-discipline and spiritual clarity. Meditation, on the other hand, enables one to cleanse the mind of clutter and distractions, fostering inner peace and serenity. Similarly, prayer serves as a means of purifying the spirit, allowing me to surrender my ego and connect with the Divine.

Furthermore, purification ceremonies involving the use of sacred substances such as incense, herbs, or holy water are prevalent in various cultures. These rituals often involve smudging or sprinkling these substances to cleanse the aura and sanctify the environment, creating a sacred space conducive to spiritual awakening and clarification.

My journey towards enlightenment has been fraught with challenges and obstacles, many of which stem from the complexities of my human psyche and the distractions of a material world. Personal cleansing serves as a potent tool for navigating these challenges, offering a means of purifying my inner landscape and aligning me with higher truths.

On a psychological level, personal cleansing promotes emotional healing and psychological well-being, allowing me to release pent-up emotions and traumas that hinder my spiritual growth. By confronting and processing these inner conflicts, I am able to shed my limitations and attain a state of inner peace and equilibrium.

In addition, personal cleansing fosters a sense of reverence and humility towards the Divine and the universe, acknowledging the interconnectedness of all beings and the sacredness of life itself. This profound shift in perspective enables me to sacrifice ego-driven desires and attachments, embracing a path of selfless service and philanthropy.

I remained in the womb of nothingness until the ego was no more, only Love remained. Whether it took a millennia or a couple of seconds didn't matter, as time does not exist in the nothingness. Time, I realized, was a strong ally and a major tool of influence used by the ego to control people's activities. Love usurps all!

"When I return, what will my purpose in life be?" I asked the void.

"Take an extra hour to help the children and your neighbor when you see them in need. Help an animal when you see them in stress or struggling. Help an elderly person tie a shoelace or guide them across the street.

"Too much of your life has been focused on achieving goals. The Divine isn't concerned with achievements, just the kindness and compassion in your heart. When you act out of kindness, you have already realized the purpose in life. You don't need to look any further; be kind to yourself, your brother and your environment.

"The purpose in life is the same for everyone. No one has a different purpose than another. As Picasso stated, 'The meaning of life is to find your gift. The purpose of life is to give it away.' It all begins with kindness."

And then, all became quiet again.

# Chapter 13

## The Beatitudes

*"Be of service to your fellow man and you will serve God. Life is about giving, not receiving."*

*"One cannot proclaim the Fatherhood of God while ignoring the brotherhood of man."*

*Urantia Book*

I felt myself tumbling down as eons of time passed before me, coming to rest in the labyrinth. Before opening my eyes a vision appeared before me. I was in the back of a great multitude of people eagerly listening to a speaker in the distance. Though at least 100 yards away, I could hear his tender voice clearly. It was Jesus, with a dynamic energy, speaking to the multitude his Sermon on the Mount. I could clearly hear him say from Matthew 5:8, "Blessed are the pure in heart, for they will see God."

It was then that I opened my eyes. Everything was radiating before me. The trees and rocks, even the sky became a brilliant white with subtle blue and lavender hues. I've never seen the northern lights, but I was sure they were not equal to this spectacle before me. I knew in an instant what lay before me, what I must do. The words of Jesus were meant to be shared. His message was universal; meant to be shared with all mankind. I realized there was still much I needed to learn as I continued my journey within the labyrinth.

As I closed my eyes to continue listening to Jesus' message, these words formed within my heart, "Blessed are the poor in spirit, for theirs is the kingdom of heaven." I instantly recognized the importance of humility and simplicity while realizing my spiritual bankruptcy. Divine Grace can only be achieved once ego and pride have been surrendered. Through humility and simplicity our hearts open to the spiritual richness and the eternal acceptance of the Grace of God. I fell to my knees praying that I might embrace the human state of humility, helping me to recognize my spiritual grandeur.

Another message followed shortly after, "Blessed are those who mourn, for they shall be comforted." I remembered my period of grief and mourning after losing my son and how it began to help me look within, strengthening my own internal fortitude. By embracing my pain and acknowledging my worldly disconnects, I began to develop compassion and empathy for myself, and others. Through personal suffering I found peace and comfort in the presence of God, whose Love helped me overcome the trials and tribulations encountered on this earthly plane.

Next came, "Blessed are the meek, for they shall inherit the world." Often perceived as a weakness, being meek, in spiritual terms, incorporates strength under control through a gentle and kind personality that abstains from any type of aggressive nature. We align ourselves with Divine Energy once we relinquish the need for power and control. For it is within the blessing and richness of God where we find fulfillment.

Yet another message formed within my heart, "Blessed are those who hunger and thirst for righteousness, for they shall be filled." Moral integrity and justice, I realized, lie deep within the human psyche and one must pursue goodness with renewed energy to align one's actions with the beliefs and principles of love, compassion and equality. In doing so, one becomes spiritually fed and satisfied. Our souls are spiritually replenished when we realize the fulfillment of God's promise.

"Blessed are the merciful, for they shall obtain mercy." Divine

Love is unconditional, offering forgiveness, mercy, and compassion to everyone regardless of their deeds. As is God, so should we be! Do not resent or hold animosity towards anyone, regardless of their behavior. Instead come from a desire of reconciliation and healing relationships. God will bless us with unconditional love and peace and joy.

I could feel my heart filling with love as another message entered it, "Blessed are the pure in heart, for they shall see God." Devote your life to God and His will through purity, integrity, sincerity, and acceptance. When our hearts are pure we will see the world around us in a different light. We will learn through the suffering and despair and come to realize only goodness and joy exist in the Divine Presence. Our inner transformation and spiritual acceptance instills a spiritual clarity helping us to recognize that, "All is God."

The next message came immediately following, "Blessed are the peacemakers, for they shall be called sons of God." As there are no conflicts within the Divine, so should we work to avoid conflicts within ourselves and with our brothers and sisters. Through forgiveness and working towards peace, we help create an earthly environment where love reigns and differences are overcome, helping to foster unity, understanding and acceptance. Simply resolving conflicts is not enough; peacemaking transcends conflict resolution by restoring harmony and acceptance. To walk the path of righteousness, one must practice and understand that our true reality is Love. Love is all there is!

One final message came to me, "Blessed are those who are persecuted for righteousness' sake, for theirs is the kingdom of heaven." It takes courage to proclaim God's message and to forgive and forget for there will be those who will judge and persecute you. One must be strong in faith and assured in their commitment to spread the word of God. Knowing one's Truth is imperative in transcending societal norms and beliefs, for Spiritual Truth will always surpass the truth of man. Bearing witness to the Love of God is the highest elevation in consciousness one can achieve.

Slowly I opened my eyes as my heart was still pounding from

the deep spiritual insight I had just received. I recognized them as the Beatitudes Jesus presented on his Sermon on the Mount. They are as relevant today as they were back in the ancient days as they present principles of spiritual growth centered on humility, simplicity, compassion, forgiveness and righteousness. I realized these are not religious doctrines, but they are a bedrock of spiritual, offering a means of inner evolution and awakening.

By embracing these concepts, individuals opt to let go of their material necessities while *Becoming* messengers of Divine Love, working towards making positive changes in their lives, their communities, and the world. I realized these simple concepts challenge the very fabric of our earthly lives, which are predicated on the ideals of separation and individual concepts and needs. I prayed that I might be strong enough to spread the Love.

I came to the realization that these timeless truths surpass religious boundaries, while offering guidance for spiritual awakening and awareness. Through humility, compassion, righteousness, and perseverance, one is invited to embark on a journey of inner transformation, leading to a deeper understanding of themselves, their relationship with others, and their connection to the Divine. As one embodies these virtues in their lives, they become instruments of God's love and agents of positive change in the world, ushering in the Kingdom of Heaven on earth.

As I continued to navigate the labyrinth, I came to understand, God doesn't only show up in me or other people; No, God shows up in everything and everyone we see around us. We are surrounded by the glory of the Divine! Every blade of grass, every insect, every thought, every instinct, every, everything has its root foundation in the All That Is. Like the trees bearing fruit, giving their gifts of apples, pears, oranges, coconut, etc. without the obligation of any return. Their fruits feed people, birds, animals and even the earth itself when their fruit falls to the ground. They are the instruments of God giving; they are the instruments of God's love showing up.

We, too, are instruments of God; we, too, distribute God's love.

And how do we do that? Our gifts to our brothers are different for and from individuals depending on the circumstances entering our presence. One time it looks like compassion, another time it looks like forgiveness, another time it's giving thanks, it also shows up as money for the poor, food for the hungry or clothes for the homeless. Realize, however, that you are the instrument through whom God shows His love, as Jesus said, "My Father doeth the work."

Every moment of every day, God shows up through us bestowing blessings upon blessings to everyone and everything in this great universe. He/She asks nothing in return; He/She doesn't judge or punish. God knows only Love. God is Love. Our only function is the recognition of our *Being* and spreading the Love throughout this planet. Love is an incomprehensible richness that cannot be matched in this tangible world; it is the answer to all conflicts. Once Love has been experienced one will never be the same and the only victim will be the ego.

God is the gift that never stops giving. Our physical world, I grew to understand, is one giant organism ebbing and flowing in response to the highs and lows of individual expression. I remembered a prayer Jannette, my wife, delivered at church several years ago:

"Right here and right now, I know that that presence of the Divine is all there is. That Presence is absolute unconditional Love and Grace. That is the presence that flows through me and is me. There is no other presence in my life. I just know that as I unite with this presence and know that it is my partner in life, that I have nothing to fear nor worry about. I am so protected and safe that I   release the need to have any outside protection of armor. That presence of Love, of my Creator, is my protector. I am not alone. I stand united with Absolute Love. My heart is surrounded and enveloped in this Love. I release anything that is not centered in this Love.

"With this knowing, I am able to look within myself and feel and know the Love that the Divine has for me. It's the

Love that was there when I was created and born. I am that Divine idea of God in the Flesh and so, when I speak my Word, I know that it is coming from that Divine Part of Me that is absolutely Perfect. I stand in my Truth and am able to do so in Love and Kindness. I speak my Word with Love and Kindness. I know that I am that Divine Vessel of Love and I allow Spirit to speak thru me and as me. I step aside and surrender and allow Spirit to speak It's Word thru me. I let my ego know that it is safe and that Spirit has this. It doesn't need to protect me. Spirit is taking care of that now.

"I also recognize and feel the Love that Spirit has for me. As it's child, I now know that I am Loved and as the Vessel of the Divine, I stand in my Truth as Myself and I know that I do so in Love.

"I just give such great thanks for the remembrance that Spirit and I are One. I am not alone and never have been and I give thanks for that. I also give thanks for the manifestation of my Word.

"I release this prayer, I release my Word, with the absolute faith and  knowing that it is already done in the mind and heart of the Divine One. And so with  great  gratitude,  I  let this go, I let this be, and I ground it by declaring,

And So It Is!"

It's power and meaning overwhelmed me to the point where I repeated it twice. Tears of joy traced my cheeks as I became aware of my spiritual growth. My heart was finally open to receive. It left me with the realization: that which I'm seeking, I already am. There is nothing to search for, nothing to ask for and nothing to forgive. Prayer is simply a means of communicating with my internal Self, a means of opening the heart channel to who I really am. *Becoming* is actually nothing more than awakening, realizing who I really am.

But it wasn't just an awakening, it was much more than that; it was an acceptance and an embracing of my true nature. By realizing who

I truly am, I'm also realizing who I'm not. Once I accept my spiritual nature, there comes a realization there cannot be duality and oneness; omnipotence, omniscience, and omnipresence embody the oneness. Letting go was never about relinquishing material gifts but rather surrendering to the spiritual Truth within.

Once accepted, I needed to develop an internal, value-based roadmap to ensure I would not falter by the wayside. *Believing* and *Becoming* are preliminary steps to *Being* and, in that sense, can be easily usurped by continued daily influences. Building an internal dam to block egocentric needs and desires is, therefore, an important building block in maintaining my focus on my spiritual rebirth.

Self-discovery was essential to continually nurture my newfound spiritual awareness. What would keep me from falling off the wagon? I began to mentally formulate a list to help me maintain and strengthen my spiritual beliefs:

Maintain and encourage an inner dialogue and thoughts understanding the importance of introspection and self-reflection.

Constantly continue to be kind to yourself and others.

Understanding past experiences will not only help you let go of their negative effects, but will help in developing a solid foundational belief system.

Intuition is important in guiding one to a greater spiritual development. Listening to your internal Self will help to discard external events.

Building a solid connection with others will help your spiritual resolve, especially compassion and empathy.

Rise above your physical self while embracing the mystery of the spiritual.

Knowingly continue to live within your spiritual Self.

Nothing, however, can match the serenity of going inside; here is where the true Inner Christ resides. Prayer no longer becomes an activity of searching for the Divine outside of oneself, instead there comes the realization where prayer becomes that communication from within, not directing, but receiving. As such, prayers can never be rote; they are simply a means of opening the heart to receive. And once the heart is open to receive, prayer becomes a way of life, a mechanism by which one maintains a constant contact with the Divine. Every word becomes a prayer, every act becomes a prayer and every thought becomes a prayer. It is through prayer that one maintains a constant contact with the Inner Christ. By embracing this continuous contact one allows the Inner Christ to flow outward in self-expression.

Only when prayer becomes a continuous act of *Being*, can consciousness rise to the level of enlightenment. Enlightenment is, quite simply, acknowledging the Divine in every facet of one's life. And so it is. It was at that instant I realized there was more to *Becoming* than to simply go inside and open one's heart. It was a pre-requisite to understanding and embracing life in the universal whole. Everything matters, from the tiniest of atoms to the galactic enormity. Existing in this enormity lies brotherhood. It brought me back to a time when Malachi was teaching a class on brotherhood.

As I entered the classroom at the Academy of Lifelong Learning, Malachi was writing on the white board. It was a mathematical formula, "Brotherhood = Acceptance + Forgiveness." This was followed by the very well known Biblical phrase, "Love thy neighbor as thyself," with one small caveat, neighbor was lightly crossed out and above it he wrote brother/sister.

"Hi," I said as I entered the room, "I guess today's class is about brotherhood."

"Based on what you see on the white board, I can understand how you can surmise that but, in reality, today's class is really about ourselves. How we feel about ourselves is the precursor to how we feel about others. Once we understand and come to accept our Divine Oneness, then our love for our fellow man is an automatic by-product. One cannot love their brothers unless one truly loves themselves."

"It's difficult to achieve in this world with all of the different ideals permeating this planet, different religions, different races, different eco-socio standard, different political views and so on and so on," I replied.

"Exactly! So how do we fight through all the obstacles to achieve unity? It's not about giving in to our ideals to accept someone else's, but it's all about how we view ourselves and who we think we really are."

I noticed the chairs were placed in a circular fashion instead of the usual horseshoe shape and asked why the change.

"This way we can all see one another and no one is in the front or back. At God's table we are all equal," Malachi replied.

By the time he finished his reply, several students were already seated with a couple more following closely behind. "Good morning everyone," Malachi began, "today we're going to discuss brotherhood, what it means, how it evolves and why it's important. Does anyone care to take a stab at it?"

"Brotherhood is the elimination of personal biases and treating everyone as equal," one student began.

"Good, anyone else?"

"Brotherhood is the total inclusion of all people into one globally united community," another offered.

"Very good, anyone else?"

"To me it's simply an act of acceptance, not just allowing people to be different but also embracing their differences," a third student offered.

"That's critical," Malachi began, "how can we profess brotherhood when we don't embrace the differences within people? Are we not all different? We all think differently, act differently, look different, so why do we extrapolate differences due to race, politics and religion and judge those people to be unworthy of our acceptance? How often have we heard it said that my fellow Coloradoans are my brothers but not the Mexican immigrants residing here? What about Conservatives placing a negative label on Liberals, and vice versa? But before we can truly define brotherhood, where does it start, Hans?"

Hesitating a bit, I finally replied, "From within, where everything starts."

"OK, so you're saying it's more of an 'Innerhood' instead of a Brotherhood?"

One of the students interrupted, "Doesn't it depend on our definition of brotherhood? Is brotherhood an acceptance and recognition of equality with the people who share this planet with us, or is brotherhood that internal spiritual love we attribute to God?"

"You tell me," Malachi was quick to respond, "is there, or rather should there be a difference between the two?"

"I don't believe there should be a difference," the student claimed, "if we are truly children of God then there shouldn't be a difference at all. We are all equal in the eyes of God."

"There was a quote in *The Urantia Book*," I interjected to support the student's claim, "One cannot proclaim the Fatherhood of God while ignoring the brotherhood of man."

"That sounds all well and good," another said, "but it depends on who we think we are. If we're a physical species then we are by nature judgmental and will continue to define brotherhood according to the filters of our value system. If we are spiritual beings immersed in the Love of God then we cannot be anything but loving and accepting."

"Bravo!" Malachi let out a yell, smiling broadly, "You hit the nail on the head, Hans you were on the right track but you faltered in the stretch run. Everything starts with us and therefore the most important decision we can ever make is to determine who we really are. Are we physical beings spending a limited time on this planet only to return to the dust whence we came? Or is our reality spiritual in nature owing our existence to the Love of God and, thereby, embracing every being as our brother in a realm that knows no other way? Who believes our roots are derived from the spiritual nature of things?" Malachi stopped to survey the room, "Come on, raise your hands if you believe your true nature is spiritual rather than material."

Slowly I raised my hand, the others followed suit. "So, how do we get there?" someone asked.

"By understanding who you really are!"

There was a moment of silence as, I suspect, everyone was thinking about who they really are and whether this scene before us, the classroom, the teacher and the students were real enough. "What about forgiveness, how does that fit into all of this," someone asked, breaking the silence?

"That's an interesting question, one would think that brotherhood and forgiveness go hand in hand. But we have to be careful here. Too many people believe that brotherhood and forgiveness do go hand in hand, that true brotherhood includes forgiving your brother for whatever you may not agree with. In that sense, we create a system of inequality. Having to forgive someone for whatever you don't agree with doesn't make them equal to you. Brotherhood is based on freedom! Each individual is free to choose their own life journey, unencumbered and, this is the kicker, without judgment. Forgiveness, more often than not, is self-imposed. All too often we feel the need to forgive someone when the actual need for forgiveness lies within ourselves. Brotherhood is more appropriately based on equality and acceptance of which forgiveness is a byproduct but not the main steering mechanism."

"So forgiveness doesn't play a role in brotherhood?" I interjected.

"I'm not saying it doesn't," Malachi began, "I'm saying that forgiveness plays second fiddle to acceptance and equality. Not that forgiveness is not required, as you can see, I've included it in our brotherhood formula, but it's not the primary focus. I see forgiveness of self playing a larger role than forgiving others."

"Why is that?" I asked.

"Forgiveness of others is predominantly based on personal judgment, and judgment has no place when it comes to brotherhood. Embracing your fellow man in his endeavors and lending a hand whenever necessary is of primary importance. Don't judge what he's doing or how he's doing it. Brotherhood is about acceptance not tolerance; there's a big difference here. Let your neighbor define who he is, don't define him yourself, that's judgment. Remember, while forgiveness is important, the primary focus of forgiveness is on the self. You can only change yourself, not others. Everyone is different; there are no two people alike. You can see that by looking at your own household, your son, your daughter, your spouse, your relatives, your friends, etc., etc., etc. Accept their differences and their choices, don't judge how they do it or why they do it; bless them, support them and wish them well. And always remember, God has no favorites; His love is unconditional regardless who you are or what you do."

"But what about sin?" I continued.

"Sin is self imposed judgment created by the absence of love in our material world. Remember, God is Unconditional Love and knows no sin. He sees us all through a loving light that holds everyone as perfect and complete. If there were any sin against God it would be our perception of separation, but even that cannot be true, regardless of our beliefs, so there are no sins against God. Sin was created in our world of form and was created by judgment and greed. Forgiveness of sins, therefore, is primarily an act of self-contrition which helps us rid ourselves of guilt and fear."

"Then why does the church require the forgiveness of sins before one can be saved?"

"It's actually not required. We are already saved because we are one with God. Contrition and the resulting damnation or heavenly resurrection is a doctrine that has been supported by the church body for hundreds of years. We can all guess why, but that will more likely than not take us too far off the subject at hand. Suffice it to say, we will all bask in the Love of God once our earthly time has come to an end. God's unconditional love will ensure everyone's salvation."

I smiled as I returned to my labyrinth and continued walking the path. With all of the complexities life has to offer and the apparent distance of our spiritual connection, our mysterious spiritual nature was rather quite simple, as Jesus said:

"And thou shalt love the Lord thy God with all thy heart, and with all thy soul, and with all thy mind, and with all thy strength: this is the first commandment. (Mark 12:30)

"And the second is like, namely this, Thou shalt love thy neighbour as thyself. There is none other commandment greater than these." (Mark 12:31)


The clarity of *Becoming* was fully presenting itself. Life's perceived complexities were nothing more than our failure to realize our connection to the Divine. Difficulties arise as we continue to separate ourselves from who we really are. All of man's established rules can be simplified to the words Jesus spoke. Loving yourself and your neighbor equally and completely while realizing we are all Divine beings is living in constant prayer, living in constant communion with Divine Love.

As I continued to walk slowly along the labyrinth's winding path, I felt a major shift in consciousness. The repetitive motion of walking became meditative, inducing a state of focused attention and heightened sensory awareness within me. My mind was becoming attuned to the present moment, fully immersed in the act of walking. With each step, I became more attuned to my surroundings, noticing the texture of the ground beneath my feet, the play of light and shadows within the trees, and the gentle rustle of the breeze. This heightened awareness fostered a sense of mindfulness, allowing me to be fully present in the here and now.

As I approached the center of the labyrinth, a sense of anticipation began to build within me. This journey inward mirrored the inner journey of my soul, leading towards a deeper understanding of the self and the divine. With each turn of the labyrinth's circuits, I shed layers of ego and illusion, thereby drawing me closer to the core of my *Being*. Waiting at the center of the labyrinth, representing a sacred space of revelation and transformation were profound insights and spiritual revelations. Here, in the stillness of the center, where boundaries between self and others dissolve, I was looking forward to experiencing a profound sense of unity and interconnectedness with all of creation.

Upon reaching the center, I paused to rest and reflect, savoring the moment of stillness and serenity. In this hallowed space, the veils of illusion were lifted, and the true nature of reality was revealed. I experienced a profound sense of clarity and insight, as I was bathed in the light of Divine Wisdom. Here, in the heart of the labyrinth, lay the discovery of a deeper sense of purpose and meaning, fully aligning within me the awareness of divine purpose that guided my journey.

# Chapter 14

## The Transfiguration

*"If he have found his centre, the Deity will shine through him, through all the disguises of ignorance, of ungenial temperament, of unfavorable circumstance. The tone of seeking is one, and the tone of having is another."*

Emerson

As I was preparing to retrace my steps out of the labyrinth, I felt a presence and saw two glowing lights descend from above, coming to rest next to me. It was Malachi and Teacher coming to welcome me home.

They were no longer physically recognizable; instead they were gradients of energy whose form and expression changed with each telepathic message. Their colors were a soft green mixed with white and lavender. Hues of gold and orange hinted to the majesty of their spiritual expression. They merged and separated at will giving rise to their universal oneness. Though not physically recognizable, their spirituality was ever present and their individualized consciousness was unmistakable. Their telepathic communication was more understandable than our vocal language in the physical realm, as it included the feeling of all senses, while including the tranquil energy of peace in one unmistakable message. And within it all was the ever presence of Love which dominated the encounter and added a euphoria unknown in this world.

"You have completed your cleansing. While your mind is still dormant and your heart open, you must come to realize that once you let go of your past, you will embrace a new consciousness, you will be resurrected to a new Hans."

"Yes Malachi, I understand."

"Then you must also realize that your path to *Becoming* has not yet been fully realized. There is still much to do."

"Yes Teacher, I know."

I began to pray.

*In this sacred moment, I humbly come before you with a heart open to receive your boundless grace and wisdom. As I stand at the threshold of spiritual awakening, I surrender all attachment to materialistic ideals that have clouded my vision and distanced me from your eternal truth.*

*I release the grip of worldly possessions, knowing that true fulfillment lies not in the accumulation of wealth or possessions, but in the richness of the soul. Help me, dear Creator, to transcend the illusion of materialism and embrace the abundance of love, compassion, and spiritual growth that you offer abundantly.*

*Grant me the strength to let go of the distractions that have veiled my consciousness and prevented me from recognizing your presence in every moment of my life. May I walk the path of enlightenment with courage and determination, trusting in your divine guidance to lead me towards the light of truth and understanding.*

*Fill my being with divine light, illuminating the dark corners of my mind and dispelling the shadows of doubt and fear. Awaken within me a deep sense of inner knowing, so that I may discern the difference between fleeting desires and the eternal essence of my soul.*

*Help me to cultivate a spirit of gratitude for the simple blessings that surround me each day, recognizing that true*

*wealth resides in the beauty of nature, the kindness of others,
and the infinite love that flows through all creation.*

*Guide me to seek solace in the silence of meditation, where
I can connect with the depths of my being and commune with
your divine presence. May each moment of stillness bring
me closer to the realization of my true nature and the
interconnectedness of all life.*

*Grant me the wisdom to recognize the sacredness of every
living being, treating each with kindness, compassion, and
respect. May I embody the virtues of humility and service,
using my gifts and talents to uplift others and contribute
to the greater good of humanity.*

*Help me to release all judgment and expectation,
embracing each experience as an opportunity for growth and
self-discovery. May I surrender to the flow of life, trusting
that everything unfolds according to your divine plan, even
in the face of uncertainty and adversity.*

*As I journey deeper into the realm of spiritual
enlightenment, may love surround me like a gentle embrace,
comforting me in times of darkness and inspiring  me  to
shine my light brightly for all to see.*

*In your infinite mercy and compassion, hear my prayer
and guide me ever closer to the truth of your divine presence.
Amen.*

My mind re-visited my approach to the center of the labyrinth,
where my sense of anticipation began to build, where I was prepared
to bid my farewell to my special guides, Teacher and Malachi. My
journey inward mirrored the inner journey of my soul, leading towards
a deeper understanding of the Self and the Divine. With each turn of
the labyrinth's circuits, layers of ego and illusion fall away, drawing me
closer to the core of my *Being*. At the center of the labyrinth, I knew,
lay a sacred space of revelation and transformation, where profound
insights and spiritual awareness are encountered. Here, in the stillness

of the center, the boundaries between self and other dissolve, as I experienced a profound sense of unity and interconnectedness with all of creation.

As I reached the center altar of the labyrinth, I relived being bathed in Light. It wasn't a normal light, but one filled with Divine Love and Peace and Joy. I was enveloped in the *Being* we call God. This *Being* not only surrounded my whole self, but it was equally present within my true Self. Everything was Light; everything was Love; everything was Peace; everything was Joy! Both inside and out! Here, at the heart of the labyrinth, lay a deeper sense of purpose and meaning, aligning Divine Oneness with purpose of Inner Self, as my true nature and reality are revealed to me. Here I pause and reflect, embracing this moment of stillness where the veil of illusion is lifted to resurrect my true Self.

Unable to hold myself back, I fell to my knees. To be surrounded by such grandeur was the ultimate *Being*. It required nothing; It wanted nothing, while It gave everything! But I was not only bathed in Light, my own essence was glowing in Light. I knew I was not alone, Malachi and Teacher, in their spiritual splendor, were still beside me. Their words of wisdom were no longer required as their energy of wisdom and truth flowed freely and uninterrupted amongst us. All was understood without anyone speaking a word; all was received without anyone giving; all was complete. It was simply a co-mingling of energies and vibrations. It was the ultimate letting go. It was the resurrection unknown to mankind, from without to within!

Malachi and Teacher, I knew, would no longer guide me for I had reached the stage of material freedom, finally understanding my Truth: I am one with all there is! I am Love! I am Peace! I am Joy! There was nothing else to understand, there was nothing else to learn! Slowly Malachi and Teacher faded away, never to be seen again in my material world, while always being present within my spiritual one. I came to understand that oneness and nothingness were both gradations of something and, as such, were the same thing. The complexities that lay within human understanding had simply withered away, being replaced by a higher spiritual Truth. My lifetime illusion of a material world wrought with problems and confrontation no longer existed. My material truth had given way to my Spiritual Truth!

To complete my transformation I had to come to terms with the Universal Oneness, embracing all there is as an experience of the Divine. Nothing, I realized, was separated or isolated from the Whole, everything glowed from the Light of Divinity. Letting go was not a simple process of changing my life, but it required a concentrated effort to embrace that which was God, not necessarily embrace it, but *Become* it! Only a rise in consciousness would create a new Hans; only a rise in vibration can resurrect one to a higher consciousness.

Still being a member of the objective world, I was preparing myself for criticism and ridicule by those who were still mired in a world of separation. I would have to garner up the strength required to not falter from my newly formed beliefs in the wake of dogmatic realities, which all too often clashed with the reality of Spirit.

It reminded me of a meditation many years ago where I saw the loving image of Jesus in all its glory, spreading love that moved my inner soul. Slowly this image changed and became the hated terrorist Osama Bin Laden. Yet it was not the hated terrorist the world had vilified, instead he was as glorious and loving as was Jesus. This vision reinforced my belief that deep within the self lay a Self centered within its own Christ nature waiting to be brought forth, waiting to be resurrected.

With this vision came the realization that my meeting with Malachi and Teacher, in the center of the labyrinth was, in a sense, my Transfiguration, an acknowledgment of my true Spiritual reality. All three of us were bathed in a loving Light, bestowed in peaceful Grace and filled with eternal Joy. "And he was transfigured before them, and his face shone like the sun, and his clothes became white as light." (Matthew 17:2)

"God places us in the world as his fellow workers-agents of transfiguration. We work with God so that injustice is transfigured into justice, so there will be more compassion and caring, that there will be more laughter and joy, that there will be more togetherness in God's world. " (Desmond Tutu)

I had reached a point where faith was no longer needed or viable. I had reached a stage where faith was forever replaced by a glorified knowing. For faith is the ultimate stage of *Believing*, while knowing begins the transformative process of *Being*.

Transitioning from a material to spiritual consciousness marks a profound shift in perspective, one that far surpasses the superficial trappings of the physical world and delves into the depths of the soul. It is a journey of self-discovery, inner exploration, and spiritual awakening, where I have realigned beyond the pursuit of external possessions and achievements to seek a deeper connection with the Divine.

Initially, the journey within involves the recognition of the limitations in materialism and the pursuit of external gratification. In the material consciousness, I was driven by desires for wealth, status, and power, believing that fulfillment could be found through the acquisition of worldly possessions. However, as I embarked on my spiritual path, I came to recognize the fleeting nature of material wealth and the emptiness of superficial pursuits. I began to question the meaning of life and seek a deeper sense of purpose beyond material success.

Delving deeper into the journey within, I was able to cultivate a sense of introspection and self-awareness. Turning my gaze inward, I began to explore the depths of my own psyche and confront the shadows and complexities of my inner world. Through practices of meditation, contemplation, and self-reflection, I uncovered hidden layers of conditioning, fears, and attachments that have kept me bound to the material realm. This process of self-discovery was accompanied by moments of insight and revelation, as I came to understand the true nature of my being beyond the limitations of the ego.

My next stage of the journey within involved a shift in values and priorities. I began to gain clarity about my innermost desires and aspirations, and began to align my actions with my spiritual ideals. I prioritized qualities such as compassion, gratitude, and service to others over the pursuit of personal gain. Material possessions lost their hold on me as I recognized that true fulfillment comes from nurturing the soul and fostering deeper connections with others and the Divine.

Along the journey within, came the experiences, moments where I rose above my material desires in order to hasten my spiritual awakening. These moments often happened unexpectedly, during moments of stillness and contemplation, and through encounters with nature, art, or profound teachings. In these moments, my boundaries of the self dissolved, as I experienced a profound sense of unity with all of creation. I experienced a glimpse of the interconnectedness of life and recognized the presence of the Divine in every moment and every being.

As I continued to deepen my spiritual practice, I began a process of inner transformation and integration, cultivating qualities such as love, forgiveness, and acceptance, while embracing both the light and shadow aspects of my being. Letting go of old patterns of thought and behavior that no longer served my spiritual growth, I opened myself up to new possibilities and experiences. Through this process of inner transfiguration, I became a vessel for Divine grace, radiating love and compassion out into the world.

My journey from material to spiritual consciousness was a deep and transformative process that unfolded in stages. It involved the recognition of the limitations of materialism, a cultivation of self-awareness and introspection, a shift in values and priorities, and moments of transcendence and spiritual awakening. Ultimately, it was a journey of self-discovery and inner transformation, leading to a deeper connection with the Divine and a more meaningful and fulfilling way of life.

The true meaning of the Transfiguration of Jesus, however, is simply the internal transitioning from a material to spiritual consciousness. It is a state where faith is no longer required, where faith has become a knowing. Here doubt does not exist, here Love is a way of *Being*.

My eyes remained closed as I began to retrace my steps out of the labyrinth. I knew the directions the path would take and the closed eyes helped me to maintain my internal focus. Everything was perfect as each moment of Now presented itself. I was not the same person who entered this labyrinth a few minutes ago; my internal awakening was guiding me in ways my external senses could never imagine. I saw without looking, I breathed without inhaling, I felt without touching, I spoke without talking and I heard without listening. Everything reacted like a beautiful and perfect Mozart symphony.

Within my awakening lay the realization that prayer was never a means for making requests of a God outside oneself, but a way of conversing with the Inner Self. Prayer is not a situation of asking but to listen and ultimately *Being*. Once prayer becomes a continuous act of *Being*, consciousness rises to the level of enlightenment. At that point every act or thought becomes an act of prayer, it is the only way to communicate with the Divine on a continual basis. Prayers can never be rote, they are moments of opening one's heart to Divine Source. Once that process becomes a way of life, one will have finally transfigured to the Christ consciousness.

As I neared my completion of the labyrinth, an internal message crossed my mind, "Your journey of *Becoming* will never end for the Divine is dynamic, never static. As it changes so will you, as it grows so will you. The journey to *Becoming* spiritual is an ongoing process as you continue to evolve, learn, and deepen your spirituality throughout your life."

"I understand. I am, I always am!"

# Chapter 15

## A Day in the Life of *Becoming*

*"When He was born into a carpenter's family, He was the Son of Man. When He opened His heart, the door of Heaven was opened to Him."*
Thich Nhat Hanh

Love Is! To truly *Become*, one has to understand Love. There are no degrees or levels of Love! It's all Love! There are only levels of consciousness, which determine one's ability to access the vibration of Love.

Unconditional Love is all around us. It is our consciousness, or level of awareness, which allows us to experience it. This Unconditional Love is what we call God; this Unconditional Love is energy in its highest and purest form; this Unconditional Love is a vibration present throughout the universe at every level of *Being*.

When we add, "I am," we add consciousness, a level of understanding, thereby limiting our perception of Love. By raising one's consciousness, one increases and enhances one's Love experience. Love never changes, consciousness does! Awakening is simply the act of raising one's consciousness, thereby opening one up to a greater experience of Love.

One cannot love someone more than another! One can only be conscious of it. Consciousness is limiting! Everyone loves to the level of one's own understanding, or consciousness. Meanwhile, the energy and vibration of Love never changes, never falters.

Once we understand the power of Love, or lack thereof, we are able to comprehend why there is both goodness and evil in our world; it's all driven by our embrace of who we really are. Are we bound by material values, which dictate our actions, or are we embracing spiritual values? Both are bathed in Unconditional Love, but the limiting consciousness of the material mind is incapable of reaching for a higher good. To do so one has to raise their Spiritual consciousness in order to access a higher Love vibration.

Raising one's consciousness is, therefore, paramount in both Spiritual growth and recognizing a greater Love. In fact, Spiritual growth and accessing a higher Love vibration are both the same thing. As one grows Spiritually, one opens themselves to Love. To traverse the journey of *Becoming*, therefore, one needs to awaken to a greater Love by growing their consciousness. Consciousness is dynamic, ebbing and rising to the flows and effects of a material world. *Becoming*, then, is simply the act of growing one's consciousness. With this conscious growth comes a greater understanding and greater access to the vibration of Love, a resurrection of a new you!

Are you prepared to grow your consciousness and become a new you? Are you willing to let go of who you are today to become who you really are? Are you willing to change your life and the world?

It begins, quite simply, by being kind, to yourself and others. It begins, quite simply, by embracing and filling each moment that presents itself with kindness. Be good, do good and think good becomes a new, daily mantra.

"Kindness is a simple, organic feeling that we need to awaken and grow in our hearts. We must first learn to be kind to ourselves so that we can show kindness and feel it toward others...Every one of us has the capacity to love and be kind to all other sentient beings, but we often don't try to tap into our heart's full potential. We don't realize that we are only utilizing a small percentage of our heart's potential for love."
(Nawang Khechog)

To lay your daily groundwork, begin each day with a simple prayer:

*Divine Energy, as the sun rises and fills my world with light, let it also fill my heart with kindness, humility, and happiness.*

*Grant me the strength to approach this day with kindness, to see the beauty in every soul I encounter, and to spread warmth through my words and actions.*

*Teach me the virtue of humility, to recognize my own flaws and limitations, and to treat others with respect and understanding. Help me to remember that true greatness lies not in power or status, but in the service of others.*

*Fill my heart with happiness, O God, for you have given me the precious gift of life and the opportunity to make a positive difference in the world. May my joy be shared, bringing smiles to the faces of those around me.*

*Bless this worldwide community, dear Lord, with unity and harmony. May we lift each other up, support one another in times of need, and celebrate each other's successes.*

*Guide me, Divine Love, in all that I do, that I may walk in your ways and bring glory to your name. Amen.*

Then prepare yourself to be kind through humility and simplicity. The humble mind does not want; it only seeks peace and joy for all mankind. The simple mind is not grandiose; it takes what it needs and shares the rest. Kindness does not require a higher education, it lies inherent within every living being, fostering positive thinking, creating meaningful mantras and continually letting go.

Positive thinking is, perhaps, the simplest technique to realize, yet the most difficult to achieve. Unfortunately, the mind is continually active, creating a steady stream of random thoughts. Replacing each negative thought with a positive one can be difficult and time consuming, in addition to taking one out of the moment of Now. Proactively viewing each moment through peaceful, caring and joyful filters helps one to reduce random, negative thoughts. While it may take a while to successfully create positive moments, continued repetition will eventually produce the internal habits necessary to do so.

Another way of creating kind mindsets is through the repetitions of meaningful mantras.

> "When habitual thoughts come up from your samskaras (impressions stuck in the mind), you don't have to fight with them or even replace them. You just shift your consciousness onto the mantra. With positive thinking, you are continually using your will to neutralize negative thoughts with positive ones. With mantra, you are simply using your will to shift the focus of your consciousness from the samskara-generated thoughts to the mantra." (Singer)

Mantras do not have to be deep or meaningful sayings, they can be single words like Jesus or God or Love. Using mantras throughout the day will prepare you for the moment something unforeseen happens that will upset or anger you. As you recall the mantra, your awareness shifts, allowing the event to be dealt with more constructively.

Letting go is not a one-time occurrence, but a continual practice as new moments pass before you. There is always a tendency to judge, analyze, forgive or involve oneself with events presenting themselves. Viewing what is happening before you, without any kind of involvement, is the basic concept behind letting go. Judging, analyzing, forgiving or involving oneself creates short or long-term memories, which can lead to additional issues further down the road. "Let go and let God" is a powerful mantra when faced with the challenge of letting go.

In his book, *Living Buddha, Living Christ*, Thich Nhat Hanh presents his own, personal view of the Five Precepts of Buddhism. These five precepts or five rules of training are the most important system of morality for Buddhists constituting a basic code of ethics to be respected by followers of Buddhism. The Five precepts are meant to develop mind and character, enabling progress to enlightenment. Keeping the five precepts forms part of regular devotional Buddhist practice, both at home and at the local temple. Society upholds the Five Precepts through ceremonies whereby monks lead assemblies reciting the Five Precepts. The recitations follow ancient customs.

The First Precept pertaining to the reverence of life, acknowledges the suffering and worldwide destruction of life, and realizes that in order to practice non-violence, we must first learn to act peacefully ourselves. Through mindfulness, the practice of peace, we can begin to transform turmoil within the world community and ourselves.

*"Aware of the suffering caused by the destruction of life, I vow to cultivate compassion and learn ways to protect the lives of people, animals, plants, and minerals. I am determined not to kill, not to let others kill, and not to condone any act of killing in the world, in my thinking and in my way of life."*

The Second Precept is the practice of generosity. The practice of generosity includes giving of material resources, helping people to rely on themselves and not creating fear.

*"Aware of the suffering caused by exploitation, social injustice, stealing and oppression, I vow to cultivate loving-kindness and learn ways to work for the well-being of people, animals, plants, and minerals. I vow to practice generosity by sharing my time, energy and material resources with those who are in real need. I am determined not to steal and not to possess anything that should belong to others. I will respect the property of others, and I will prevent others from profiting from human suffering or the suffering of other species on Earth."*

The Third Precept deals with responsible sexual behavior. Sexual misconduct has destroyed many families and individuals. One needs to realize that sexual communion is a bonding of body and spirit. It is the ultimate expression of love, a deep, beautiful and whole union of body and spirit. It is a shared experience where people open their vulnerability to another. These encounters bring the deepest feelings to the surface. It is the highest form of love a person can experience on the human level.

> *"Aware of the suffering caused by sexual misconduct, I vow to cultivate responsibility and learn ways to protect the safety and integrity of individuals, couples, families, and society. I am determined not to engage in sexual relations without love and a long-term commitment. To preserve the happiness of others, and myself I am determined to respect my commitments and the commitments of others. I will do everything in my power to protect children from sexual abuse and to prevent couples and families from being broken by sexual misconduct."*

The Fourth Precept deals with speaking and listening deeply. This precept includes not telling the truth, exaggerating, misrepresenting what others said, and filthy language. At the core of this precept is the understanding that words can destroy friendships and relationships. By speaking in a wholesome and loving way, we help to dissolve barriers and prejudices that prevent us from being mindful when we talk.

> *"Aware of the suffering caused by unmindful speech and the inability to listen to others, I vow to cultivate loving speech and deep listening in order to bring joy and  happiness  to others and relieve others of their suffering. Knowing that words can create happiness or suffering, I vow to learn to speak truthfully, with words that inspire self-confidence, joy,*

*and hope. I am determined not to spread news that I do not know to be certain and not to criticize or condemn things of which I am not sure. I will refrain from uttering words that can cause division or discord, or that can cause the family or the community to break. I will make all efforts to reconcile and resolve all conflicts, however small."*

The Fifth Precept deals with what we eat. We believe our bodies belong to us, forgetting we belong to the Oneness. Whatever we do to ourselves, affects the entire universe, just as the effects of the entire universe has helped in the creation of you. "To keep yourself healthy in body and mind is to be kind to all beings."

*"Aware of the suffering caused by unmindful consumption, I vow to cultivate good health, both physical and mental, for myself, my family, and my society by practicing mindful eating, drinking and consuming. I vow to ingest only items that preserve peace, well-being, and joy in my body, in my consciousness, and in the collective body and consciousness of my family and society. I am determined not to use alcohol or any other intoxicant or to ingest foods or other items that contain toxins, such as certain TV programs, magazines, books, films and conversations. I am aware that to damage my body or my consciousness with these poisons is to betray my ancestors, my parents, my society, and future generations. I will work to transform violence, fear, anger, and confusion in myself and in society by practicing a diet for myself and for society. I understand that a proper diet is crucial for self-transformation and for the transformation of society."*

Mindfulness is an awareness of what is happening around you. It is by being aware that we become motivated to act through understanding and compassion. Once embarking on the spiritual path of *Becoming*, one not only embraces an internal change, but that internal change manifests itself in affecting external change as well. One cannot change internally without affecting change to the world around them. Spirituality comes in a package deal, to be shared with everyone.

Begin the day with a simple prayer:

*"Divine Love,*

*As the morning light breaks through, I come with a humble heart and an open spirit. Grant me the strength to live this day with purpose, guided by love, equality, and kindness.*

*May I see the beauty in every soul I encounter, recognizing the inherent worth and dignity in each person. Help me to treat others with compassion and respect, embracing diversity and celebrating differences.*

*Grant me the wisdom to seek equality in all my actions, advocating for justice and fairness in every corner of the world. Let me be a beacon of hope for those who are marginalized or oppressed, working tirelessly to create a more inclusive society.*

*Fill me with kindness, so that I may extend a helping hand to those in need, offering support, comfort, and understanding without judgment or discrimination. Let my words and deeds spread warmth and positivity wherever I go.*

*Guide me on this journey, Divine Love, as I strive to make a difference in the lives of others and leave a legacy of love, equality, and kindness. Amen."*

Go forth on this day without purpose, let its events flow into your presence without judgment, spreading kindness to whomever or whatever you encounter. Remember to do good and be good and think good in everything you say and do, without exception. Look before you and around you and see the Divine Love that exists in everyone and everything. Come from the heart. While you are eating, be grateful, not only for your meal, but for everyone who helped to bring this meal to you: the farmer, the truck drivers, the cooks, the animals, and plants.

When you're walking, are you walking kindly? When you're thinking, are you thinking kindly? When you're talking, are you talking kindly? Smile at the people you pass on the street and wish the merchants you interact with well. Try to heal a strained relationship. Give help to the needy. Be grateful for your natural surroundings, realizing that the shining sun and drenching rain are gifts of the Divine necessary for the enrichment of the planet.

Breathe in the fresh air deeply, marvel at the beauty of the wild flowers, listen to the song of the wind, feel the wonderment of it all! Realize, it's all God, from the tiniest insect and blade of grass to the tallest majestic trees. See the Divine Essence within everyone, including yourself. Become aware that nature is a uniform system within the Oneness working in unison to benefit every living being on the planet. Fully understand that whatever you do, affects not only you, but everyone around you as well.

Should a bad thought enter your mind or a trying event enter your space, do not react harshly or angrily. Rather, go within and search for a kind solution, humbly accepting blame if necessary or forgiving if needed. Regardless of the circumstance, kindness is the theme for the day. Spread kindness to everyone!

When you go to sleep at night, don't look back and relive the day. It will only take you into the past, over which you have no control. Stay present, stay within and end your day with a prayer of gratitude:

*"Divine Love,*

*As the day comes to a close, I bow my head in gratitude for the kindness that has filled my day.*

*Thank you for the opportunities to show compassion, for the moments of connection with others, and for the love that has been shared.*

*As I reflect on the day's events, may I carry forward the*

*warmth of kindness in my heart, letting it guide my actions and interactions tomorrow and always.*

*Grant me the humility to acknowledge my shortcomings and the courage to grow from them. Help me to forgive myself, and others, for any shortcomings or misunderstandings that may have occurred.*

*As I prepare for rest, may I be filled with peace, knowing that I have done my best to spread kindness in this world.*

*Bless those who have touched my life today, and bless those who may need kindness tomorrow. May we all strive to create a world where kindness reigns supreme. Thank you, Universe, for the gift of another day. Amen."*

# Chapter 16

## Living Prayer: A Map of Transcendence

*"Great is the soul, and plain. It is no flatterer, it is no follower; it never appeals from itself. It believes in itself."*

Emerson

I have reached a stage in my life where prayer is no longer a part of my life; it is my life! Every thought is a prayer! Every action is a prayer! Every spoken word is a prayer! It is so because I'm in constant contact with my Inner Self.

Judgment has been let go some time ago as I now watch events unfold before me without involving myself unless absolutely necessary, and if my involvement is required I ask how I can infuse the Higher Good into what is unfolding before me. To the best of my ability, I interact in every event with kindness. If necessary, I forgive and let go.

As best as I can, I live by ten core values, realizing we are all "Divine Beings!" As expressions of a loving God, love and goodness exist in our DNA. Therefore, we do not become Divine Beings; we awaken to our calling. Once my calling was realized, I formulated a set of principles that I have embraced and live by. These values are enhanced and solidified through insightful prayer and dedication. Here are my ten core values:

• Awareness:

Once Spirit entered my being, I understood it was time for my awakening; it was time to begin my journey home.

Before I could begin my journey as Divine Being, I needed to realize I was, by nature, loving and caring. My inherent pedigree recognized and preferred positive and caring relationships. Relationships were not only sought with others but I became aware that I needed to establish a relationship with my inner self as well. Love and caring, I understood, did not begin outside myself, but must be established within. Once I began to feel comfortable within my own identity, I was able to replace my outer self with an inner Self that continues to bring a loving and caring message while building lasting relationships. My journey began by going within! Constant awareness of who I am is required to build a lasting spiritual base, requiring me to move my focus from the mind to the heart. It becomes imperative not to let external events dictate my actions, but rather for my internal convictions to influence and direct my outer actions.

"Knowing yourself is the beginning of all wisdom." (Aristotle)


• Forgiveness:

Once I was able to embrace a life centered on forgiveness, I was able to pierce the walls of bias.

After coming to terms and forgiving myself for my imperfections, I began to understand this imperfect world was filled with imperfect beings. It is, therefore, imperative to expect less than positive reactions and experiences, as some may become downright ugly. Forgiveness, therefore, plays a major role. As a spiritual being, I must realize the imperfections present in any situation and I must be prepared to forgive, not only the people around me but, more importantly, myself as well. I strive to remember that forgiveness always begins with the self. People who cannot forgive themselves will, inevitably, not be able to forgive others.

"If we really want to love, we must learn how to forgive." (Mother Theresa)


• Non-Judgment:

I have learned to applaud the effort and not question the means.

As a temporal being I realized that I was in a constant state of judgment of people, situations, etc. As my spiritual consciousness grew, I began to understand that everyone is built differently, thinks differently, and prioritizes differently. Letting go of judgment, therefore, includes allowing everyone to create their own lives in their own ways, and always being ready to lend a helping hand whenever needed. Once I realized that every being has its roots in Divine Love, letting go of judgment was imperative because it placed obstacles in the psychological and spiritual growth of others.

"Judging a person does not define who they are...it defines who you are." (Unknown)


• Empathy:
 I have learned to open my heart to the feelings of others.

Do not feel sorry or pity for another, for that is sympathy. Rather, understand and share the feelings of another, for that is empathy. Understanding how another feels as they travel along life's circuitous road enables my true Self to provide meaningful support to others.

"No one cares how much you know, until they know how much you care." (Theodore Roosevelt)

• Gratitude:
I am grateful for all that has been bestowed upon me.

Being grateful creates an internal humility that does not begrudge others nor does it create jealousy. Being on the road to enlightenment, I understand and appreciate the journey and am not concerned with what I do or do not possess. Gratitude is not a fleeting emotion that comes and goes, it is a state of *Being*.

"Wear gratitude like a cloak, and it will feed every corner of your life" (Rumi)


• Acceptance:
Embrace your brother, regardless where his journey takes him

Understanding and knowing who you really are is the bedrock to universal brotherhood. Under God, all men are created equal and no man should be judged otherwise regardless of their differences. All of God's creations, myself included, are begotten from unconditional love and we all share a connection to that Divine Energy.

"One cannot proclaim the Fatherhood of God while ignoring the brotherhood of man." (*Urantia Book*)

• Giving:

"It is more blessed to give than to receive." (Acts 20:35)

The real power of giving comes from a selfless act of simply giving from the heart. This act is not tied to any special event or celebration. It is merely a time when I choose to give from the heart because I want to share and show my appreciation for who we truly are. Giving is not merely monetary, but also includes volunteering and sharing goods. The motivation behind giving is love and strengthening my relationships with others.

"For it is in giving that we receive." (Saint Francis of Assisi)

• Truth:

Awaken to the Truth and fulfill your life

Truth is never a practice or belief, truth is a knowing! By living my authentic self I bring happiness and joy into everyone's life. I realize that the truth of this world is different than the Truth that is God. My truth lies in the connection to God and His creations, the Oneness. Embrace the Truth that is No Thing, the realization of our Spiritual reality.

"Never be afraid to raise your voice for honesty and truth and compassion against injustice and lying and greed. If people all over the world...would do this, it would change the earth." (William Faulkner)

• Peace:

Embrace the Peace, which surpasses all understanding

The power of peace dwells within us all. I allow my inner calm to dictate the outer events attempting to influence my life. Peace is more than the absence of conflict or state of rest, peace is the inner wholeness connected to Divine Source. It is the partner of Truth and together they form the cornerstone to Love, which encompasses all.

"Do not let the behavior of others destroy your inner peace." (Dalai Lama)

"Nobody can bring you peace but yourself." (Ralph Waldo Emerson)

• Love:

There is only Love

I know love as a strong, personal commitment, desire or attachment to an individual or some other tangible connection. This type of love is not all encompassing as the Love of God is. Love, in its essence, is a state of *Being*. Love, along with Peace and Truth form the spiritual triumvirate that is God. Live Love and live God.

"Let us always meet each other with a smile, for the smile is the beginning of love." (Mother Theresa)

Adyashanti, in his book, *Resurrecting Jesus*, lays out a Map of Awakening. It is a formal compilation of the *Becoming* process as he sees it.

"The journey of awakening to the divine *Being* that you and I can realize internally, Jesus lived out in his life story, through his humanity...In order to understand the (Jesus) story being told in the Gospels, you literally need to absorb it, to *Become* it. You can't remain a spectator and expect to understand it, because then you're on the outside, still stuck in the logical, linear mind. The truths being conveyed through the Jesus story are beyond logic, beyond the conditioned thinking mind; they're of a higher order of wisdom that you can only really understand by awakening." The path of *Becoming* is the path of awakening. While each person will ultimately forge his or her own path, there are some basic stages everyone will encounter.

The "Calling" is the first stage of awakening, arriving when one initially feels that spiritual impulse, which grabs their attention. This calling can arrive at any time in their lives in a variety of forms. It is the point when the daily activity of life begins to look at a higher purpose and meaning of life. It often comes with the realization that there's more to life than a daily, mundane existence determined by needs and wants.

Spiritual "Awakening" occurs when one realizes their normal state of outward consciousness has moved to one's deep, internal true nature. There's an actual shift from one view of reality to another. There's a major shift from seeing life as outside of one self to embracing the internal oneness and realizing the interconnectedness of all beings. Letting go of old standard beliefs marks the beginning of one's spiritual journey.

"There are many degrees of awakening, but *all* awakening has as its common denominator a shift from seeing ourselves as a separated, isolated human beings to seeing ourselves as that which we all share. You can call it consciousness, divine *Being*, spirit, God. Many words can be used, but it's the experience that matters."

At some point after the awakening, questions and doubts will rise to the forefront of your mind. This is a period of "Trials and Tribulations," which can be short term or long term and will put your new-found beliefs to the test through situations you encounter, testing the very foundational values of your new realization.

"As we go through our trials and tribulations, outer circumstances seem to be exquisitely put together specifically to test each part of our realization...You could think of these inward and outward trials as a form of purification. You're purifying the vehicle: body and mind, the same body and mind that you woke up out of when you awakened. Now this vehicle has to undergo its own purification so spirit can fully embody your humanity." (Adyashanti)

Once one's period of trials and tribulations come to an end, one's inner *Being* is finally free of all conflict. The "Abiding Tranquility" that follows, is the inner state of unification: your psychology, your spirit and your will. Once internally unified, one cannot help but to see the outer unification as well. They are, after all the same thing. When this unification occurs, life becomes simple, leading to a deep sense of freedom, well-being and fearlessness.

Ultimately, the abiding tranquility opens one up to the fullness of *Being*, the radiance from the tips of your toes to the top of your head signals the oncoming "Transfiguration." There's a realization that God is inside you. "It's not your ego that realizes it's God, but your true essence." (Adyashanti)

With it comes the realization that everything matters, every pebble, every insect, and every blade of grass. Our physical world is one giant organism, ebbing and flowing, in response to the highs and lows of individual expression. At this point the ego has fully fallen away.

"Relinquishment" is, quite simply, the death of the ego. When a part of your ego or identity dissolves, an attachment to the external physical world is also dissolved. This occurs because, up until this point, you relied on the external world to fulfill a need. It very likely remained unconscious until this point. At this point, you have gained enough inner strength to take the forced leap to let go of that aspect of yourself. When you do this, you will stand alone with a partial loss of identity. No words can explain this feeling.

Until one has moved beyond the ego, one is still at the micro level of consciousness. At this level one may be *Becoming* aware of the universal connectivity of all there is, consciousness is still thought of as a personal awareness, as separation has yet to be fully embraced. It doesn't diminish the ecstasy of enlightened consciousness as it has not yet attained Divine Consciousness, which can only be reached once the ego is fully discarded. Macro, or Divine Consciousness is the conscious connection of all things, spiritual and material. Consciousness at this stage is so powerful that all *Beings* share their energy of Love, which is constant throughout the Universal Oneness, where no one is greater than another. As one approaches the attainment of Macro Consciousness, one also releases their individual personality. It's like a tree shedding it's leaves who become the source of further growth for the tree.

But the process is almost always in stages. To have a complete loss of identity all at once, in Adyashanti's opinion, would not be survivable.

The stages, depending on the level of suffering, will dissolve the ego layer by layer. Each time losing an attachment to the physical world and thereby losing hope from the external physical world. It is a place of gaining further inner strength. These stages involve tremendous feelings of hopelessness, which simply means you have attached to the external world but it has been a false hope. The hopelessness disappears once you have the strength to stand on your own and be willing to face any more suffering alone.

You will understand that you have never been alone, as you will sense the unseen spiritual world surrounding you. It understands you, it supports you, and it loves you unconditionally. The further you dissolve your ego, the stronger you will feel alone in this physical world, but the door will open further to the spiritual realm.

Within "The Transmutation," life takes on a whole new direction. One's outlook is completely selfless; you have lost all sense of self. "At that point, really, the only thing left to do is to be a selfless, benevolent presence in the world - there's really nothing else to do, nothing else that makes sense." (Adyashanti) This is where the journey of awakening ends. *Becoming* has been completed, as *Being* is all there is left.

The process of *Becoming* shows us we are two sides of the same coin. "We are all God appearing as man and as woman, divine *Being* manifesting as human being." (Adyashanti) Only our mind and experience separate our humanity and divinity. Our whole spiritual journey has, therefore, been the awakening of the realization they're not separate. They never have been!

As we become the personality we were meant to be, we realize that there are internal powers growing within. These are not physical or mental powers, but spiritual strengths becoming known to us, which slowly change our view and understanding of who we really are. These so called powers are actually Spiritual gifts available to everyone, everyone who has embraced their internal soul while discarding the cloak of the ego.

Our Power of Oneness illuminates natural wisdom that makes it far easier to see what matters in life and what doesn't. It enables us to bask in a sense of worthiness, belonging, and beauty. In short, it helps us see and experience the true meaning of our connection to all that is.

The spiritual Power of Equality is a profound concept that transcends societal norms and material distinctions. At its core, it recognizes the intrinsic value and dignity of every being, regardless of external differences in race, gender, status, or beliefs. The spiritual Power of Equality is altering and liberating. It invites us to overcome superficial differences and embrace the deeper truth of our interconnectedness. By embodying equality in our thoughts, words, and actions, we contribute to a more harmonious and compassionate world.

The Power of Reflection, coupled with contemplation, invites the Holy Spirit into our personal and professional lives through a purposeful, focused prayer life, devoted to bringing God with us into every moment of our journey. Reflection illuminates one's knowledge, assumptions, and worldviews, playing a crucial role in personal growth. It involves critically assessing past events, understanding lessons learned, and applying these insights to future situations.

The Power of Creating is an intense expression of our divine essence and purpose. When we engage in acts of creation—whether through art, innovation, or nurturing relationships—we tap into a fundamental aspect of our spiritual nature. Creation is a sacred endeavor that connects us with our divine nature and the larger net of existence. It invites us to embrace our innate creativity, cultivate mindfulness, and contribute to the co-creation of a more compassionate and harmonious world.

Through the Power of Choice, what we choose to believe determines what plays out in our lives. One of the most amazing faculties we have in this dream is our power of choice. If we decide to be happy no matter what, our attention automatically begins to shift toward the source of happiness within, even in the midst of intense circumstances.

The Power of Compassion, together with empathy, viewed from a spiritual perspective, heals by recognizing the divine within each person. These acts transform toxic emotions, replace negativity with understanding and kindness, and lead to a life of eternal bliss by realizing the universal manifestation of the Divine.

The Power of Perfection invites us to embrace our wholeness and interconnectedness with the universe. It encourages us to rise above limiting beliefs and cultivate a state of inner harmony, authenticity, and loving-kindness. Ultimately, spiritual perfection is about embodying our highest potential and contributing to the collective evolution of consciousness. In spiritual terms, perfection often refers to the inherent completeness and purity of our divine essence. It suggests that at the core of our being, we are whole and interconnected with the universal source of creation.

The Power of Healing, in a spiritual aspect, refers to spiritual energy working at a deep level in our spiritual being. The healing involves the transfer of energy; in other words, it is not from the healer himself or herself, but the healer links with 'Universal' or Divine energy to channel healing for the mind, body and spirit.

The spiritual Power of Individuation is a reflective process of self-discovery and inner growth that leads to the realization and embodiment of one's unique essence and purpose. Individuation, as a concept developed by Swiss psychiatrist Carl Jung, refers to the psychological journey of integrating unconscious elements of the psyche into conscious awareness, ultimately leading to a more whole and authentic self. It is a sacred journey of self-discovery, integration, and authenticity that leads to greater wholeness, purpose, and alignment with the Divine within and around us. By embracing individuation, we awaken to the beauty and uniqueness of our soul's journey and contribute to the unfolding of a more conscious and harmonious world.

In religious experience, the Power of Transcendence is a state of being that has overcome the limitations of physical existence, and by some definitions, has also become independent of it. This is typically manifested in prayer, rituals, meditation, psychedelics and paranormal "visions." The spiritual Power of Transcendence opens the doorway to sincere spiritual growth, awakening, and realization. It liberates us from the confines of the ego and material world, inviting us to embrace higher states of consciousness, love, and wisdom. Through transcendence, we align with the eternal truths of existence and contribute to the evolution of individual and collective consciousness.

The journey from *Becoming* to *Being* represents a passionate transformation of consciousness and being. It involves a series of inner processes and shifts that lead to a deep and lasting connection with one's spiritual essence. The journey towards spiritual *Being* is a life altering progression of consciousness characterized by self-awareness, healing, expansion, and alignment with spiritual values. It culminates in a state of intense presence, peace, and service to the greater good, embodying the timeless truths of the spiritual journey. While *Becoming* is an evolutionary path to spiritual awakening, it is, through the development of *Being*, that we fully embrace our Divinity.

# Being

*"You can't re-merge with something or someone that you've never been truly separated from. However, you can emerge from your sleeping state, your belief in separation, or the illusion of separation, and realize what has always been true - that you are one with God."*

James Twyman

# Chapter 17

# My Spiritual DNA

*"The beauty of Life itself is alive and well within me. It connects me with every other being, as we are created into existence from the same One. As spiritual beings we share the same spiritual DNA."*

Jane Beach

We are in a constant state of *Being*. What one is *Being* at any particular instant is determined by their consciousness. One cannot be what one is not aware of. One cannot be sad if they're in a moment of happiness. Consciousness is the dynamo that feeds the internal engine of life; personal conscious awareness is an ever-changing process driven by internal emotions and external events. Consciousness drives the engine of evolution.

The energies of omnipotence, omniscience, and omnipresence are all around us and to the degree that we can tap into those energies determines our state of *Being*. It must stand to reason, therefore, that *Being* is dynamic; every moment is unlike the next, just like every experience is unlike another. No greater example of this can be given than the Hawkins levels of consciousness, which states that conscious ranges at the personal level vary from "shame" at the low end to "enlightenment" at the high end. One can, therefore, understand that a life lived in "shame" is vastly different than one lived in "love."

It's consciousness that connects all things to the Divine Oneness. Within consciousness resides Spiritual DNA that can be found in all things. Spiritual DNA is a concept that intertwines the metaphysical with the biological, suggesting that just as we inherit physical traits from our ancestors, we also inherit spiritual attributes, tendencies, and potential. This idea hypothesizes that our spiritual essence is imprinted with a unique code, much like our genetic makeup, and this code influences our path, purpose, and experiences in life. Exploring this concept requires delving into the nature of spirituality, consciousness, and the unseen forces shaping our existence.

Understanding spiritual DNA begins with recognizing we are more than our physical bodies. We are beings of energy, consciousness, and spirit. This perspective aligns with the teachings and spiritual philosophies that emphasize the interconnectedness of all things and the existence of a universal consciousness or divine intelligence. In this view, our spiritual DNA is a thread connecting us to a higher level of existence, carrying the imprints of our soul's journey across lifetimes.

The notion of spiritual DNA suggests that just as our physical DNA carries the information necessary for the development of our bodies, our spiritual DNA contains the information necessary for our spiritual development. This information includes our inherent talents, predispositions, and lessons we are meant to learn in this lifetime. It encompasses the karmic patterns and spiritual gifts passed down through generations, as well as the potential for growth and enlightenment we carry within us.

One way to understand spiritual DNA is through the concept of karma. Karma refers to the law of cause and effect, where our actions, thoughts, and intentions create energy that influences our future experiences. According to this belief, our spiritual DNA carries the imprints of past actions, shaping our current circumstances and opportunities for growth. These karmic imprints can manifest as challenges or blessings, guiding us towards the lessons we need to learn to evolve spiritually.

"Peacefully and vibrantly alive in me, my soul guides
me when I pay attention. It's like a trusted friend, one that

knows my questions before I ever ask them, leading me to the answers I seek. Always available to me, It's my inner wisdom,  my spiritual essence. When I don't know what to do, it's the part of me that does know...With my willingness to pay attention to the wisdom of my soul I can change my thinking, my attitude and behavior. It has nothing to do with the other  person, as I'm the one who wants to have peace in my life. It takes practice! I celebrate my growth when I remember and am gentle with myself when I forget."

Jane Beach

For instance, someone might find themselves repeatedly facing similar challenges in their relationships, finances, or health. From a spiritual DNA perspective, these patterns are not random but are deeply rooted in the soul's history. They are opportunities for healing and transformation, encoded in our spiritual DNA as part of our soul's blueprint. By recognizing these patterns and addressing them with awareness and intention, we can shift our karma and alter the trajectory of our spiritual journey.

Another aspect of spiritual DNA is the transmission of spiritual gifts and abilities. Just as we might inherit artistic talent, musical ability, or athletic prowess from our ancestors, we can also inherit spiritual gifts such as intuition, healing abilities, or a strong connection to the Divine. These gifts are part of our spiritual DNA, waiting to be awakened and developed. They often emerge naturally as we align with our true selves and our spiritual path, revealing the unique contributions we are meant to make in this lifetime.

The activation of our spiritual DNA is closely tied to our level of consciousness. As we raise our awareness and expand our consciousness, we begin to access deeper layers of our spiritual DNA. This process often involves shedding old beliefs, healing past wounds, and cultivating a higher vibration through practices such as meditation, prayer, and mindfulness. As we do so, we unlock the potential encoded in our spiritual DNA, allowing us to live more authentically and in alignment with our soul's purpose.

A critical aspect of this process is the understanding our spiritual DNA is not static; it is dynamic and responsive to our thoughts, emotions, and actions. Just as our physical DNA can be influenced by environmental factors, our spiritual DNA can be influenced by our spiritual practices, intentions, and the energy we cultivate. By consciously engaging in practices that elevate our vibration and deepen our connection to the Divine, we can activate and transform our spiritual DNA.

In my own spiritual journey, I have found that embracing the concept of spiritual DNA has provided a framework for understanding the deeper patterns and potentials in my life. It has encouraged me to look beyond the surface of my experiences and to see the larger aspect of my soul's journey. This perspective has brought a sense of purpose and meaning to my challenges, as well as a deeper appreciation for the gifts and talents I have inherited.

For example, I have always felt a strong intuitive sense and a deep connection to nature. These qualities, which I now recognize as part of my spiritual DNA, have guided me towards a path of spiritual exploration and healing. They have also helped me to understand and navigate the karmic patterns in my life, providing insights and guidance, which have been invaluable on my journey towards enlightenment.

Spiritual DNA is an inherent concept highlighting the interconnectedness of our physical, emotional, and spiritual selves. It suggests our spiritual essence carries a unique code, which influences our path, purpose, and experiences in life. By understanding and embracing our spiritual DNA, we can awaken our inherent gifts, transform our karmic patterns, and align more deeply with our soul's purpose. This journey of awakening and transformation is at the heart of the spiritual path, guiding us towards greater self-awareness, fulfillment, and enlightenment.

# BELIEVING BECOMING BEING

**********

Everything has purpose, or why would it be? From the tiniest atom to the great expanse of the universe, everything that is, needs to be. For if it didn't need to be, it would quickly be ignored and disappear. From the vast expanse of something to the presumed void of nothing, everything contributes to the great omnipresence of all there is. Nothing is wasted, nothing is ignored; everything is embraced. If not by me, then by you; if not by you, then by someone; if not by someone, then by something.

In the deepest currents of human understanding, there is an underlying sense that everything, at its core, exists for a reason. When we consider the intricacies of life—from the birth and death of stars in galaxies light-years away to the countless cellular interactions within our own bodies—it's tempting to interpret these as signs of purpose. In a world where every particle, every wave, every organism seems to play a role, the question arises: Could it be that existence itself is a testament to a purposeful, interconnected whole? The very act of *Being*, of "is-ness," suggests that everything has a part to play in the cosmic symphony.

Consider an atom, a particle so minute that billions of them could align across the width of a single hair. Despite its size, the atom is the building block of all matter, forming molecules and structures that become planets, plants, animals, and, ultimately, us. The atom has a specific role to fulfill within a larger framework, and even though it might seem insignificant on its own, it contributes to the creation of all things. In this sense, it is not only necessary but essential, a reminder that small things are, in fact, foundational to larger realities.

The same understanding can be extended to the cosmic expanse stretching beyond our view, where galaxies spiral and collapse, stars are born, and black holes form and consume. These celestial processes are as necessary to the universe as the atom is to the human body. Through these vast phenomena, we witness transformation, creation, and even destruction. But this destruction is never wasteful; its energy gives way to new forms, new stars, new worlds. The cycles of birth and death, the constant flux of energy, are essential to the grand design, adding depth and vitality to the universe. They affirm that nothing is truly lost—everything merely changes, fulfills a purpose, and moves on.

Purpose, however, does not only reside in the grandeur of physical forces. It permeates every experience, every interaction, every thought and feeling that we, as conscious beings, encounter. Within our lives, seemingly mundane moments contribute to who we are. Each breath, every choice, whether profound or trivial, becomes part of our journey, shaping us and those around us in unseen ways. Just as the atom's structure determines the nature of a molecule, each of our experiences plays a formative role in the structure of our lives. This concept of interconnectedness suggests that purpose is not something outside of us, something that happens at a distance, but something woven into the very fabric of *Being*.

> "Awakening to my truth is a process. In any circumstance I can choose love and I   can be peace. I ask, 'What would love do now? What would peace do now?' and  then    listen inwardly - I will know what to do."
>
> Jane Beach

And if we expand our perspective even further, beyond ourselves, we can see purpose embedded in the relationships between all things. Imagine the ecosystems of Earth, where plants, animals, microbes, and minerals interact in a complex dance, each entity playing a part in the whole. In a forest, for example, trees do not grow in isolation. Their roots connect underground in networks of fungi, sharing nutrients and resources with one another. The decomposition of one fallen tree becomes nourishment for countless organisms, who in turn contribute to the soil's fertility, allowing more trees to grow. Nothing is ignored or cast aside; everything is used, everything has purpose. Even decay and death become vital, part of the transformative cycle that sustains life. The forest is alive in ways we are only beginning to understand, with every organism participating in the harmony of existence.

This universal interdependence and synchronicity can be likened to the omnipresence of all that is. If the universe is conscious of itself in ways we cannot fathom, perhaps each of us is a thought, a feeling, an intention within that cosmic mind. Our individual experiences, thoughts, and desires contribute to a greater whole we cannot fully comprehend. In some traditions, this idea is presented as a divine unity, the Oneness binding all things. Each soul, each atom, each blade of grass is part of an omnipresence embracing everything. Every aspect of existence is interwoven, and each has its place within the grand design, whether we recognize it or not.

Nothing is wasted because, within this view, every experience, every object, and every being contributes to a larger whole. Consider our feelings—joy, sorrow, anger, love—as waves that ripple outward, influencing the lives of those we encounter and even extending to the world around us. When we experience love, for example, it expands our capacity to understand and connect with others. This energy does not vanish once it is expressed but moves outward, creating effects we may never witness directly. Similarly, pain and suffering, though difficult to bear, often lead to growth and transformation, shaping us in ways to prepare us for the challenges ahead. This notion—that nothing is wasted—speaks to a deep, underlying intelligence, which permeates everything.

If we view purpose as something greater than our individual goals, as something intrinsic to all of existence, then we might begin to appreciate the beauty and meaning in even the smallest, most overlooked aspects of life. From the perspective of universal purpose, our lives are not isolated incidents but integral parts of a cosmic journey. Every step, every stumble, every moment of clarity or confusion adds to the whole. We may not always understand the role we play, but our presence is part of a divine unfolding.

This brings us to the question of choice and intention. When we recognize that everything has purpose, we begin to see our own role in a new light. Our decisions, actions, and beliefs become opportunities to align with this universal purpose. We can choose to act with compassion, to seek understanding, to contribute to the well-being of others, and in doing so, we participate in the grand symphony of existence. By honoring the purpose of our own lives, we honor the purpose of all life. And when we choose to ignore, belittle, or disregard any aspect of existence, we deny a piece of our wholeness. The understanding that "if not by me, then by you; if not by you, then by someone; if not by someone, then by something" is a profound reminder of our shared responsibility. We are all caretakers of purpose, keepers of meaning.

So, in this vast and often incomprehensible universe, where the tiniest atom holds immense potential and the farthest galaxy is part of a larger whole, everything is indeed embraced. Our lives, our choices, our intentions—all contribute to the omnipresence of all there is. Nothing is lost; nothing goes unnoticed. And in that understanding, we find not only our purpose, but also the purpose of all things.

# Chapter 18

## Salvation

*"How simple is salvation! All it says is what was never true is not true now, and never will be."*

Jesus' Course in Miracles

*"Salvation is not elsewhere in place or time. It is here and now."*

Tolle

*"The world began with one strange lesson, powerful enough to render God forgotten and His Son an alien to himself, in exile from home where God Himself established him. You have taught yourselves the Son of God is guilty, say not that you cannot learn the simple things salvation teaches you!"*

Jesus' Course in Miracles

It has been quite sometime since I contacted my friend Malachi, but as I'm nearing the end of my worldly existence I question what I believe many others do in the same position, namely will I continue *Being* once I transition? Salvation is the term that continues to come to mind.

I have heard about salvation for years as it promises the grace of Heaven and the acceptance of God, in spite of our sinful and evil ways. Love has been preached for centuries in a world overcome with self-serving power struggles and survival. No one, it seems, is immune to the needs for survival and the desire to live comfortably within a quiet and peaceful community.

I have lived in a world where a "me first" attitude reigns supreme and caring and empathy are secondary concerns recognized once my own house is in order. I have lived in a world where the degree of helping others is a measurement of goodness and the abuse of others is sinful. These opposites have been established over time as a measure of individual success, thereby establishing layers of separation within all facets of society. It's this type of human behavior that has instilled struggles and greed between brothers and neighbors across the worldwide stage of competitive power struggles. There is no immunity from it.

It stands to reason, therefore, that standards and values be established if for no other reason than for people to live and act civilly. As these values become more and more ingrained in society, the world drifts further and further from a unified whole towards alliances built to protect material wealth and secure environments. Judgments and biases arise as a result, creating further divisions amongst people who become less trusting of one another.

The fact that everyone wants peace and to be surrounded by love has become a fleeting ideal, rarely realized and often seen as unrealistic. What remains is mistrust and judgment focusing more on blame and less and less on forgiveness. Acceptance, therefore, becomes a long, drawn out process, as trust no longer exists.

"I hear you Hans!" it was Malachi entering my awareness.

"Malachi, it's good to hear you again." It was almost like old times yet this was different as we were having a conversation within my mind. "How does one understand salvation? Or, more simply, what is salvation?"

"Hans, salvation encompasses so much more than peaceful and loving living. Salvation is much greater than acceptance and letting go. Salvation is a state of *Being*! Nothing in this world, however good or encompassing the highest imaginable ideals known to man can equal the state of salvation. In its simplest terms, salvation lies within conscious enlightenment. Salvation is not given or earned; salvation is realized. We are all one. God's Spirit resides within all of us. Once we realize that Truth, salvation is assured.

"Let me explain by using Hawkins' scale of consciousness, and examine the conscious levels of someone approaching enlightenment and how, within this conscious growth, salvation exists. As you know, Hawkins' Map of Consciousness defines enlightenment as beginning at level 700 and culminating at level 1,000."

"It tells me that levels of consciousness exist even within enlightenment."

"Yes Hans, at the 700 level universal love and compassion are consciously realized and embraced. With that comes the understanding of the connectedness of all things within a Universal Whole. Self-realization is no longer about the individual, but includes the acceptance and sense of empathy for all living things. Qualities such as forgiveness, acceptance, unconditional love and non-judgment are exhibited, as the effects of the ego are limited. This is the stage of Universal Love. As Joel Goldsmith stated in *Practicing the Presence*:

'I seek nothing but Thee. I must know Thee whom to know aright is life eternal. Let me live and move and have my being in Thee, with Thee, and I can accept whatever else may come. What difference, then, will it make if I have a body or do not have a body, if I am healthy or unhealthy? In Thy presence is fullness of life...To seek God without a purpose is the ultimate of spiritual realization.'

"Are you saying that the ego still exists at an enlightened level of consciousness?"

"In a very minimal way. The ego's influence, while still active within, will no longer dictate the direction on one's life because enlightenment is simply a state of understanding or knowing, knowing who you really are."

"Therefore, once I know who I really am, a divine expression of God, the ego no longer exists?"

"Not quite Hans. The ego still exists, it will as long as you're still in the world of form. It falls away once you give up your physical self."

"Malachi, are you saying the ego exists only in the world of form, but not in the world of Spirit, like the soul?"

"The end of the ego coincides with the death of the physical body."

"I understand. I'm sorry for interrupting, please continue Malachi."

"Feel free to interrupt whenever you need clarification."

Malachi paused momentarily to ensure no other questions were raised before continuing. "Divine Grace is realized as consciousness increases to the 750 level. At this stage the individual realizes their life is guided by Divine Spirit; while surrendering to their higher power. Moments of divine bliss and peacefulness become more frequent as one learns to trust the inherent goodness of the universe. Goldsmith makes us aware:

'God is the intelligence of the universe, the love of the universe, the omnipresent Spirit that created, maintains and sustains the universe. God is the source of the beauty of the trees and flowers and fruits. God is the very substance of the vegetables and minerals. God is the substance of the gold in the ground, of the silver, the diamonds, and of the pearls in the sea. God it is that fills the sea with fish. God it is that fills the air with birds.'"

"We are moving from the enlightenment of the self to include the whole, all that surrounds us?"

"Yes, and once the plane of Unity Consciousness is reached at 800, the ego has been completely dissolved and a merging of the collective human consciousness has taken place. The illusion of separation has been transcended and a unity with all life forms has been realized. A great desire for compassion and serving the higher good without any self-serving need is created. Individuals at this rate have become servants of a Higher Divinity, allowing the Father to do the work through them. Goldsmith further declares:

'God is in the midst of me. Where I am God is, and God's love is forever enfolding me. God is the source of my being. God is the source of my supply, the source of the very food on my table. God it is that gives me my life's work to do. God it is that gives me the strength to perform it. 'He performeth the thing that is is greater than he that is within the world,' greater than any problem that is in the world.'

"Malachi, is it true that because the ego is a personal, individual energy, it falls away as we become more accepting of the Oneness?

"Yes, when transcending the limitations of time and space, one exists in a state of timeless awareness, a constant state of Now. Here, at level 850, one has escaped the limitations of the physical world as the state of enlightenment deepens to fuller and richer moments of deep ecstasy. The ego has lost its influence at this level, as the infinite nature of reality becomes known. From *Practicing the Presence*:

'Spirit is my true identity. I have now come out and become separate; I am no longer of the world, even though in it, and therefore, I am not subject to the world's laws. None of these human beliefs is binding upon the child of God, the offspring of Spirit, which I am. God is the source of my being; God is the activity and the law of my being, and I consciously accept that. I am not subject to man-made laws; I am subject only to grace. Thy grace is sufficient for me.'

"Pure Consciousness, the height of the human spiritual evolution is reached at a consciousness level of 900. Here lies a state of pure awareness, escaping the world of duality and separation. Oneness, in its purest form, is realized. All concepts of identity are lost, as well as time and space as a merging with the Infinite Source of all creation takes place. Goldsmith further states:

'The Christ within me is my assurance that only It has power - the Son of God, the Spirit of God in me. It will never leave me nor forsake me as long as I realize     and recognize It and as long as I live the life It tells me to live. I look to It for guidance; I look to It for wisdom. Whenever a question is presented to my mind, I look down toward my heart, and the answer comes forth in whatever form is necessary.'

"Is this the state we call heaven?"

"You arrived at heaven when you reached the conscious state of 'Love' at Hawkins' level of 500, Hans. Heaven is where Love is; hell is where Love is not."

"That seems very straightforward and simple."

"Love is simple Hans, there is nothing difficult here. The difficulty lies within your own understanding and acceptance."

"How true. How true."

"As you continue your conscious ascent to level 950, enlightenment embodies a Divine Presence. As a channel of Divine Presence, one radiates unconditional, boundless love and wisdom to all beings. Here individuals embody the highest virtues of all living things, inspiring and encouraging all humanity to awaken to their true nature as Divine *Beings*.

'Actually, there is no spiritual healing apart from spiritual living, and there can be  no spiritual living apart from the experience of God. God must be experienced; God must be communed with in our inner being. The Infinite Invisible, which we call God and our individual identity, which we call the Son are one. It is within us that a point of contact must be made so that an absolute conviction of this Divine Presence can come to us.' (Goldsmith)

"Absolute Perfection and unity with the Divine is reached at a consciousness of 1,000. There are no limitations of form and manifestation, as one exists in the ultimate reality of eternal Divine communion. Absolute truth, love and joy help to guide all beings to their divine nature. And Goldsmith sums is up like this:

'I and the Father are one, and only in my oneness with God can I have the peace that I desire; only in the fulfillment of that oneness, of that love, which exists between God and the Son of God, and between the Son of God and God; only in the realization that my heavenly Father is closer to me than breathing, and nearer to me than hands and feet, and that it is His good pleasure to give me the kingdom - only in that, does a love flow out, a love that seems to be flowing from me to God and from God back to me, but which is actually an interaction within the oneness of my being in the realization of my oneness with the Father.'"

"So Malachi, salvation is not a form of judgment where one is chosen for their lifelong accomplishments, beliefs or inherent goodness. Salvation is, quite simply, the awakening to a higher good that already exists in every human being. All that is required is the realization that everyone is a child of God and, as such, everyone is already saved."

"Yes Hans. Here's a short poem by Edgar Cayce that sums it up quite well."

"I do not know the thing I am,
and therefore do not know what I am doing,
where I am, or how to look upon the world or on myself."
Yet in this learning is salvation born.
And what you are will TELL you of Itself."

(Cayce)

It was at this point that my realization became a knowing, "We are saved! We are all saved! There will be no one left behind for we are all one, One with God. Regardless of what your life looks like! The choices you made are all gateways to experiences, experiences that will somehow lead to the greater expression of the Divine. There are no right or wrong choices with Spirit, only opportunities to grow, whatever that looks like for you. God is everywhere, regardless of your choices. Our return to Oneness has already been determined; it's the choices you make that will determine how long that return will take.

'The omnipresence of God is a divine relationship that has existed from the beginning of time, and so our work is not to seek God or to try to find God. Our work is the quiet contemplation of God's presence within us, and our prayer is the realization that there is no place where we can ever become separate or apart from God!' (Goldsmith)

"Therefore the question rising above all is, 'Is salvation real or necessary?' The answer is a simple, 'No!' We are all God's children living a temporary human experience. We are all already saved because we all come from the Oneness called God. Salvation from the Oneness doesn't make sense since it already is perfect, whole and complete. It is our belief in separation, which instills the need for salvation. And since we all exist within the Everlasting Infinite all we need to do is to become aware of who we really are. As long as we deny our inherent divinity, we will not become who we really are. Awaken, rise up and embrace your *Being*, for we are all nothing less than perfect!

"See with your heart and not your eyes. Touch with your heart and not your hands. Listen not with your ears but with your heart. Accept, never deny, who you really are! Awaken to your truth! Therein lies your salvation!"

"It is the Self that saves us from the self." (Holmes)

"The only age I know is the one that belongs to me, here and now, and here and now is the only age there will ever be. The ever present here, the eternal now and the only evidence you and I will ever have of it is our reaction to it...Our reaction to it is our salvation, not from sin or future punishment, but our salvation from our own ignorance." (Holmes)

"Very well stated Hans, there comes a time when it all comes together in one glorious Holy Moment, when everything becomes abundantly clear and obvious." Malachi began, "it begins as a moment of the self, rapidly escalating to a higher bravado as the Inner Self explodes into *Being*. That moment is so glorious and inspiring it is impossible to keep it within. At that point the body becomes a vessel and antenna, if you will, capturing Divine Love that cannot be kept within but must be shared or your body will explode. *Being* is that energy encompassing all. Therefore, when *Being* arises within it is not your personal revelation but all the energy of *Being* that exists at that moment!

"*Being* can never be kept at bay; it can never be kept within for self-experience. It rises to a crescendo of expression heretofore unknown in our lives. *Being* is all-inclusive, never partial. It is a moment so magnificent it will never be forgotten. An instant of *Being* usurps a lifetime of joyous living. An instant of *Being* encapsulates the energy of Love like never before. An instant of *Being* will forever change your life! *Being* is that moment when you realize who you really are.

"In that moment there is no ego, there is no awareness outside of *Being*; there is only Divine Truth. In that Holy Moment there is only an inner expression of immense and intense Love exploding to be shared. It is a moment of complete fulfillment whose 'cup runneth over.' This moment cannot be suppressed; it must be shared. It is never a moment for the self but a moment for the Universal Self, greater even than the Christ consciousness residing within us all. The Christ consciousness is the internal match lighting the Spiritual flame! *Being* is not for the faint hearted!

"Walter Starcke calls it "The Third Appearance," the moment the physical self merges with the spiritual Self. It is the moment of awakening. It was the moment when Jesus became the Christ. This is the same Christ residing within us all, waiting to be acknowledged, waiting to be reconciled.

'To reconcile means to bring together into a oneness. In combining Jesus' name and His title, Jesus and Christ, he was making the man and His consciousness One and the same. That tells us that reconciling the human with the divine is the true meaning of the Christ message.' (Starcke)

'I believe the progress of spiritual evolution didn't stop with Jesus. When he said, 'Greater works than theses shall ye do,' he was announcing that those who followed him would further push the envelope of consciousness. Today we are becoming conscious of the fact that humankind is as important to God as God is to humankind. They are one and the same...Consciousness is God. There has never been a God other than consciousness, and in humankind consciousness has become conscious of itself...Man is God's recognition of Himself.' (Starcke)

"Many perceive this Holy Moment as being born again. There is no such thing as being born again. One cannot become what one already is! We either forget or remember our holiness. The moment we accept time and space as a thing, a reality, is the moment we forget. This is the moment of separation. And our whole purpose from that instant on is to find our way back by coming to terms that our reality is Divine Consciousness. Those things of our world are tangible, temporary things that will eventually disappear. It is those things without form that are everlasting: consciousness, love, energy, and vibration. One must remember that our spirituality is intangible and, therefore, eternal. Our material world is tangible and, therefore, temporary.

'The perception of separation from God occurs as soon as there is the slightest notion of time and space, with the belief in time and space comes distance which separates one from another. When we see ourselves as separate beings, the concept of being more or less appears, and this is where fear and need are born. We cannot return to God because we never left God. We only had a thought that we did...You cannot move in time and space back into God. You can only move as God.' (Stewart)

"It is the great trilogy of your existence: you believe, you become and you be. This applies to all facets of life. Quite simply, we are what we believe; there is no other way. One cannot be a preacher of truth and live a life of treachery. One cannot profess to be honest and live a life of lies and deceit. One cannot profess to be pure while living a life filled with debauchery. Likewise, one cannot profess to be Christ-like without the spiritual perception of Godliness and Oneness.

'Listen. I Am in the silence between these words and lines, and underneath the very air you breathe. What I Am and who you are, are the same. We share our essential Beingness. Every heart beats with the same life force. That is the miracle and mystery of life. Let us explore our essence so that we may come to the felt  realization that who I truly am and who you truly are, are the same.' (Stewart)

"Therein lies the power of the Holy Moment Hans; it lifts the spiritual consciousness to the point where all tangible things fall away. It is the moment of Truth when the material illusion is replaced by your spiritual reality. It is the moment when separation no longer exists and you have returned to the Oneness from which you came. It is the moment when the Four Pillars of Divinity are realized, when Truth gives way to Love, when Love embraces Peace, and when Peace ascends to unbelievable Joy. It is the moment you call salvation."

'According to the Savior, after death, the human body disintegrates into the elements from which it was formed, and only the spiritual soul is immortal and lives forever. This knowledge leads people to the realization that they are spiritual beings created in the image of God, and it enables them to overcome the worldly attachments and bodily passions that lead to suffering and death. As a result, the ultimate goal of salvation is not the resurrection of the body at the end of the age, but the ascension of the soul to God, both in this life through following the Savior's teachings and at the death when the bonds between the body and the soul are loosened beyond time and eternity.' (Richardson)

"Salvation, to put it quite simply Hans, is the moment you realize and embrace your spiritual Self. It is the moment you become aware of who you really are. Salvation is the moment you become fully awake!"

# Chapter 19

# Coming Home

*"If we're one with God or an embodiment of God - or however you want to express that thought - then there's nothing we can say about the Divine that isn't also true about us."*

James Twyman

My brief journey into this spiritual universe began with a soft, feminine voice calmly whispering to me as I slept, telepathically requesting that I arise, "Hans, get up, you're dead, we have to go." I saw myself sitting up in bed thinking that I was going to praise God and see my dear deceased friends Patsy and Johnny. One final "We have to go," and I found myself longing to merge with the Light.

Initially I saw myself sleeping next to my wife before I began floating easily towards the Light, mesmerized by an indescribable sensation of euphoria. I did not think about my family who I was leaving behind. The physical world, with all of its problems, concerns and worries, were not an issue here. No adversary or ill feeling could possibly pierce this armor of joy and happiness. Here tranquility, peace and love abounded. The Light called me and I was more than willing to comingle with it. I was completely immersed in the NOW.

I could see myself, in what appeared to be a long, white flowing gown, drifting effortlessly towards the Light. This wonderful Light appeared like the rising sun, emanating brilliantly tapered illuminations from its sides until they blended with their horizon. This Light radiated warmth enveloping my entire being, while illuminating the horizon with unequaled, yet non-blinding, brightness. Above all, this radiance propagated an unparalleled sensation of love. It was the most beautiful thing I have ever experienced, the warmth, the love, the peace, the joy and the knowing, knowing this is where I wanted to be. Nothing else mattered! The Light called with an unparalleled brightness that would have been blinding in my physical world. This Light was multi-dimensional, it had warmth and feeling, it exuded peace and love; it was the first time I felt true Love. It wasn't only a feeling, it was a *Being*; my soul had emerged from its lifelong hibernation to introduce me to my true Self. I finally knew what it was like to be immersed in Divine Oneness. I was coming home! Not only did I see myself and the Light, I was *Being* myself and the Light! All my senses were activated to their extreme euphoria, all my doubts and fears of physical death were erased, all the love I could possibly bear filled me to a point of bursting and not one iota of judgment remained in my consciousness. It was love and purity in its highest form. I was no longer my physical self, I had reawakened to my spiritual Self; I had returned to who I really was.

The Light kept pulling me onward, urging me to enter a new world, a world I had long ago forgotten existed.

As I was floating towards this bright aurora, I found myself wanting to see my feet, followed by another telepathic message saying that it was not yet my time. This mental connection to the physical dimension is, I believe, what prompted my return. Why my feet? I will never know. Perhaps, after carrying me for all of these years, they felt abandoned, useless as I was floating in air. In any case, a gentle tap on my shoulder awoke me and I found myself sitting up in my bed thinking, "WOW! I was just dead." However, the tremendous sensation of love was still within me, a feeling unequaled in our physical world, an emotion so great I wanted to immediately return to my newly discovered dimension.

While emotions in our physical space can turn in an instant, this euphoria of Love would not leave me. It diminished over time and took several days to fully dissipate. Try as best as I could, this Love would not stay. From this moment on, existing in a world where peace and love were continuously overwhelmed by differences and conflict would be difficult. God had given me the gift of experiencing His Love. I'm sure it was just a small sample as I believe our physical selves could never embrace the fullness of His being; it would put us on an emotional overload.

Today was different! The Light kept pulling me onward, urging me to enter a new world, a world I had long ago forgotten about. While entering the Light was new to me, the sublime feeling of peace, love and joy surrounded and filled my *Being* with an undeniable desire for more. Without a doubt, I could linger here for eternity, but I instinctively knew greater things than these dynamic feelings awaited me. As I neared the Light and the blissful intensity increased astronomically, I closed my eyes to fully experience this divine bliss. But I continued to see without looking as a three-dimensional hologram, with me in the middle, unfolded before me.

In the first instant that the Light touched me, It erased any harm I suffered during my lifetime: physical, mental, emotional, or otherwise. It was all Love; no other feeling could penetrate its armor. I can't say how long I was floating in this bliss, because I no longer have a sense of time. But I can say that this earthly exodus was some kind of cosmic birthing canal designed to deliver me into my new existence.

As I neared the Light I could hear the music. Playing in the background I heard the most beautiful rendition of the *Stabat Mater*. Hundreds of Sirens, with their alluring voices were raising Pergolesi's masterpiece to new heights. Musical notes like these have never graced any earthly instrument. But this was not a song about Mary's sadness of losing her son, but of her joy in knowing what lay before him. Death was never meant to be mourned, it was meant to be celebrated as a new beginning; as a new you being born into Spiritual bliss! How can anyone be sad about that? One's perceived material loss is actually a rebirth into love and peace and joy unknown in the material world. Death, quite simply, is the doorway to enlightenment!

At some point in time I released my body, yet my individual personality remains with me. The surrounding bliss is not so overwhelming as to overcome my *Being*, quite to the contrary, this bliss enhances who I am and fills me with such divine knowing that I realize my eternity. While my body is no longer hindering me, my conscious self- awareness is more astute than ever before. This bliss is like being in love multiplied by a thousand, but this love has nothing to do with anyone else, it's fulfilling in and of itself.

The energy and vibration here is so intense, no human body could ever survive it. While I have yet to enter the Light, I know that this higher dimension is my true reality. Nothing in the earthly realm could ever prepare one for such a divine essence of *Being*. Here, I know, the issues and problems of the earthly realm no longer exist. Here everything is possible as there are no limitations and everything is filled with potential.

I don't know how long I've been floating towards the Light but it doesn't matter, as I'm more than content to remain in this blissful state for however long it takes. This place is not only an area of transporting souls from their earthly existence to their spiritual *Being*, but it can be described as a place of preparation, grooming one for the moment of entering the Light. My homecoming promises to be more meaningful and beautiful than my entrance cries to the world of form.

And then the curtain parted revealing a majestic, breathtaking garden. Art, nature and vivid colors provide an enchanting setting augmenting a perfumed air with fragrances of blooming flowers. The serenity and joy and peace I felt as I approached the Light increased ten fold. In the distant background the Sirens were continuing their song.

Colors of every imaginable hue lined the garden's winding path as roses and orchids of every type thrived in perfectly manicured beds and displays. Elegant marble benches and statues, celebrating the essence of the human and spiritual nature of things, were nestled within the foliage and flowers giving the entire scene a level of elegance rarely captured in the most beautiful botanical gardens. To further add to the tranquility was the gentle flow of water cascading over colorful rocks in a series of mini waterfalls. It almost seemed like the Sirens were sitting on the rocks humming their intoxicating melodies. A small wooden bridge connected the pathways on either side of the stream, as the light created mini rainbows within the flowing waters.

Birds joined the Sirens in what seemed to be an unforgettable symphony of music and song as colorful butterflies visited one flower after another. Deer, rabbits and squirrels scampered about busily attending to their chores.

Here peace, joy and love reigned as everything was perfect, just as it was meant to be. The chaos of an undisciplined, material world was long forgotten as euphoric instants of Now replaced wishful and hopeful moments of past and future.

"Here I don't have a body of flesh and blood, but one of concentrated light. I'm sure that within this light exists the blissful joy and peace that is surrounding me. Wisdom is coming from inside me and shining out in all directions as bliss pours from my heart. I don't have an actual heart, but it's coming from that area. I'm radiating love; I'm just pulsating with it." (Kagan)

Time does not exist here, there are only present moments. These moments are like an ebbing and rising ocean taking you for a ride on waves of blissful love. Looking up I notice an indescribably bright, blue light above, one that would dwarf our sun. It's size is so enormous, I cannot see it's end, and it has no harshness to it. It exudes and embraces me in a blissful loving peace, which I cannot call a feeling. This is, without a doubt a divinely inspired experience, giving me the assurance that everything I'm realizing here is true, is actually true.

While things are vaguely familiar here, it's like I'm being welcomed home. Everything here is waving with energy. There's no matter, just a loving, energy of vibration.

**********

It wasn't long before I recognized a familiar energy, filled with love and wisdom, approaching. It was my longtime friend and mentor Malachi. I ran to embrace my dear friend who had been so patient with my earthly issues of lack and separation, almost screaming, "Malachi! Malachi!"

"Welcome to *Being*, Hans."

"This place is magnificent, Malachi. Is this where everyone comes once their transition is complete?"

"No, Hans. Everyone has their own experience specifically created for them. This place should be familiar to you as you visited it many times."

"It looks vaguely familiar."

"Your heart wasn't fully opened when you visited during your meditations. It is now. You cannot only see the difference, but you can feel it, taste it, smell it and hear it as well. You are no longer limited by your lack of understanding for here everything is known to you."

"What happens now, Malachi?"

"I will guide you through the process of reuniting you with friends and family and then through your life review. Once that is complete, Teacher will instruct you how to energize yourself and prepare you for the No Thing."

"I will see Teacher again?" I jumped for joy.

"Yes. You should also realize that everything you desire is available to you, both here in the realm of Spirit or any of the inhabitable spheres throughout the seven universes."

"That could take a long time, Malachi."

"You have an eternity at your disposal, Hans."

"What is this light above us?"

"This sphere is made of light, not fire, and instead of being yellow, its white core turns sapphire as it radiates out. It's so powerful that if you were anywhere in its vicinity, your flesh would evaporate in a nanosecond. Since your new body is made from its light, that's not a problem for you. All beings on earth carry the light from this sphere within them. That's why spiritual philosophies say that we are one.

Here you see the blue-white light everywhere, in everything—in me, as well as in you. The light from the sphere propels your soul into your body when you're in the womb. It then becomes the invisible force that gives you life. And when the time is right, this same light launches your soul right up into the preparatory chamber at the moment of your so-called death.

"Everyone on earth is eternal, but people don't know it. They may sort of believe it, but they don't know it. That's because it's too much to know. Eternity is not a concept the mind can grasp. You can try to imagine it, but then, not being able to experience it, your mind says, 'Yeah, I think it's a terrific story, maybe true,' but ultimately it rejects what it cannot understand. That's because it isn't your mind that can grasp all of this. It's something much bigger and more real than your mind." (Kagan)

"Malachi, what will happen to me here?"

"The afterlife is different for everyone as there are many worlds that take many forms. Ultimately, where you go and who you meet is entirely up to you. As you know, your father's entrance was in a garden, similar to the one we're in, yet entirely different because of his vision and understanding of things. Where you are right now and where your father entered are, as best as I can describe it, Pseudo Worlds. These are worlds that mimic your human experience so that you can relate to the earthly experiences you will be revisiting. Designed for the comfort of newly arriving souls to learn to let go of their fears, fear of death, no longer inhabiting a body or fear of punishment."

"But I don't have such fears."

"Then you can bypass this learning phase and go directly to the reunion with family and friends, like your parents did. But remember, you can be in more than one place at a time, so your experiences are not limiting. Everyone will eventually see their past life experiences in three-dimensional holograms through divine filters, designed to present your earthly life in its full, miraculous magnificence."

I continued to embrace Divine Love as my essence received and returned the euphoric feeling of Oneness. There was no limit to the

Love received or given. There was no limit to the joy and peace permeating throughout my body. But it wasn't my body anymore, it was my essence; I was connected to everyone and everything. Nothing was foreign to me; everything was as it should be. I saw with a clarity I had never known before; I felt with a sensuousness I had never experienced before; I breathed with a joyfulness I never knew existed; I communicated with a simplicity and transparency unknown in the realm of form. It all seemed so easy, surpassing all understanding. Everything was as it should be, nothing was out of place; everything was perfect.

In the distance I saw several forms approaching, their auras of love extending before them. Their warmth and love enveloped me well before they arrived. I recognized them immediately, not by their form or appearance but by my conscious connection to them. Approaching were my mother and father and son and my aunts and uncles who had long ago left the earthly plane of existence. They were welcoming me home, welcoming my return to who I really was, the I Am. When we embraced, the light surrounding us grew a hundred fold as love was given and received unconditionally. Here there was no judgment or need for forgiveness for love eradicated their need. Here the ego no longer existed for this was the realm of Divine Love.

Here there was a deeper understanding of who I really was. I was no longer this individual form called Hans Benes; I was connected to the entire spirit world through the emblazoning power of Love. We all share in this love and, as a result, we all grow in this Love. I gained a clear perspective of the interrelationship of all things. Nothing is inconsequential, nothing is a lesser of the whole. I began to understand the root of all existence is Love. Omnipresence, omniscience and omnipotence were no longer difficult to understand concepts; they became simple realities imprinted in everyone's consciousness.

Freedom here was total and complete as each experience increased one's conscious level of awareness. One could travel to the edge of the universe in an instant by just deeming it so. One could experience the forces of physics and their effects on things by just initiating a thought. One could comingle with other Spirits by just inviting them in. Nothing was impossible as all possibilities were just a conscious inspiration away.

There was a life review. It was not filled with judgment or reprimands; instead it was filled with loving understanding and purpose. I realized the vast majority of my lifetime was spent in separation, isolated from the loving spirit I really was. I understood my purpose in life was to awaken to my spiritual roots and return to the Oneness. I understood everyone was on a similar journey and the bond that held us together in the spiritual world was glaringly missing in the physical realm. I understood my fear of survival usurped my alacrity for brotherhood and love.

In my spiritual home I will embrace and fully understand the Love that is God. I will further enhance my empathic abilities as I get to welcome my spiritual brothers. Attaining knowledge is a never-ending process that serves to grow Love. Understanding and welcoming this growth, I look forward to a more successful visit when I return to the realm of form the next time.

# Chapter 20

## The Morontia Mansions



*"You can't sense the Universal oneness of God without also realizing it within yourself."*

James Twyman

After my entrance to, what I can only describe as the Garden of Eden, and my reunion with my dear earthly family and friends, as well as my life review with Malachi, I was ready to reunite with my dearest friend Teacher. As I sat on our usual white, marble bench I looked around to see what else might await me. There was nothing but what appeared to be soft, white billowing clouds. As I looked closer I could see, what appeared to be twinkling silver confetti sprinkled throughout the clouds. It was as if the clouds were attempting to connect with me.

It was just then that a telepathic message from my teacher, Teacher, entered my consciousness. "Hello, Hans, welcome back to reality!"

"Teacher, how wonderful it is to see you again." It was just then that my guide appeared from the clouds in his long, white robe. I noticed he was much taller and more slender than how I remembered him to be and he was not walking but gliding or levitating. Our embrace was brief, or so it would seem, as I have yet to familiarize myself with the redaction of time. Here, each occurrence is a moment unto itself and I have yet to understand whether each moment is a brief experience or a lengthy one. One thing I was sure of is that each moment lasted however long it needed to be.

"Teacher, why am I here? What will you be showing me?" I replied without moving my lips.

"Whenever you have any questions or need to replenish your energy levels, you can meet me here. But you don't have to be here to contact me, just close your eyes and ask your question, I will always answer."

I pondered his words for a while and then asked, "How do I replenish my energy?"

"You see that building over there?"

Just then, what seemed like a white church with a steeple disappearing into the clouds, emerged from the mist. It too appeared to be made of white marble. What was fascinating is that with everything being white, I could still recognize the benches, clouds and buildings, as each was distinguished by its own blazing white shade with its own internal mother-of-pearl hues lifting it from a mundane appearance to one of glorious splendor.

Without saying a word I headed toward the church and the doors opened for me to enter. I found myself in a large round room with a myriad of round symbols hanging on the wall. Some looked familiar like the Christian cross and the yin-yang, while others appeared foreign to me. As best as I could fathom, they were spiritual or religious symbols of varying kinds representing belief systems throughout the world, or possibly the universe. It gave credence to the fact that all belief systems, regardless of their teachings or dogmas, had their origin in Divine Providence.

My eyes turned upwards gazing into the never-ending steeple above me. I centered myself beneath it, closed my eyes, spread my arms and opened my heart. A jolt of pure energy instantly engulfed me, raising my vibration while refreshing my soul and energizing my heart. It was pure bliss. After my soul had been rejuvenated, I could feel rays of light leaving my essence and connecting with all of the round symbols ordaining the walls. This energy, I found, did not just belong to me but to all *Beings*. The energy I was feeding into the symbols soon came back to me in what became a continuous cycle of vibration bringing love and peace to the entire universe and me. The more I gave, the more I received. I learned that by giving love, I receive more love than I could ever imagine. I finally understood the Oneness joining us together in one giant embrace of love and light.

I teleported back out to the bench where Teacher was waiting for me. I didn't have to explain what had happened, he already knew. "Here your energy levels will never diminish for love is the most powerful force. Only in your material world where problems and issues continually attack the psyche will people lose their spiritual insight. One can always go within to re-energize or, if they wished, they could always visit their temple." He paused momentarily before continuing, "Close your eyes and open your mind and embrace the figure of truth and goodness appearing before you."

I did as the teacher asked and the face of Jesus, in all his glory, appeared before me. I felt calm and at ease with love flowing throughout my essence. After a while his face began to change. The beard remained but the face was no longer Jesus, it was Osama bin Laden. He was also smiling at me while continuing to fill my essence with peace and love. He was joined by the spirits of Hitler and Robespierre, then Gandhi and Mother Theresa, and soon thousands of other personalities representing all religions and political persuasions appeared. They were all basking and sharing their love. After a few moments I returned to my place on a marble bench fully energized. "Why did Jesus turn to bin Laden?" I asked.

"Everyone and everything that exists has its reality in the Divine Consciousness. Everything else is an illusion. Therefore, everything that occurs in the world of form is created within the material world where good and evil is a perception of people's objective reality. The Divine Oneness knows Its true Self to be filled with unconditional Love, where imperfection and transgression do not exist. Everyone who chooses to enter the human experience will know pain and selfishness. How one reacts to such occurrences determines their conscious growth and spiritual awareness. People with less awareness will take a longer time to complete their life purpose, often over several lifetimes. I hope you're starting to realize that lesser conscious beings will struggle through their human experience for longer periods; therein lies their punishment as they have created their own hell on earth.

"Do realize, however, that you humans have begun an endless unfolding of an almost infinite panorama, a limitless expanding of never-ending, ever-widening spheres of opportunity for exhilarating service, matchless adventure, sublime uncertainty, and boundless attainment. Your love of adventure, curiosity, and dread of monotony suggest to you that death is only the beginning of an endless career of exciting activity, an everlasting life of anticipation, and an eternal voyage of discovery." (*Urantia*)

Teacher approached closer and placed his hands on either side of my head before continuing. "Also be aware that you will grow and develop into higher consciousness levels here, in the realm of spirit, as well. Be aware this is not an evolutionary process as every possibility already exists. Growth and development is probably a misnomer, for as your consciousness continues to grow and develop, greater things will be revealed to you."

Teacher's message was filled with clarity I had never known as my inner and outer selves were no longer separate filters skewing my understanding of things, I had been born again into a new Truth. I closed my eyes and internally visualized the words and ideas Teacher was relaying. For once they made perfect sense, there were no questions or moments of doubt, only a sense of belonging and understanding the Truth. My transformation was complete! The caterpillar in my cocoon was emerging like a beautiful butterfly longing to spread its wings and fly in total freedom while enjoying the world around it. I was free at last, no longer bound by earthly bonds of rules and expectancies.

As I kept my eyes closed I could feel myself drift into a deep meditative state. Finally, I had entered the world of grace where only love, and peace existed. While my initial journey into the world of grace was filled with love and warmth, this time that feeling was enhanced with a knowing and understanding of what the Universal Oneness was all about. Omniscience, omnipotence and omnipresence were no longer concepts, I understood their reality; no, I was *Being* in their reality!

I came back to my present state when I heard Teacher. "God is a universal spirit, an infinite spiritual reality. Although invisible to human eyes, Spirits are the true universal reality. God cannot be seen in the material world because his radiance is so brilliant that mere mortals cannot gaze upon him and survive. 'The spiritual luminosity of the Father's personal presence is a light which no mortal man can approach; which no material creature has seen or can see.' Only with internal faith can the spiritual mind realize the universal Father.' (*Urantia*)

"The many planet systems throughout the universe were crated to be eventually populated by different intelligent personalities through whom God experiences Itself. It stands to reason, therefore, that these created beings have, as their primary purpose, the desire to return to their Universal Father in Paradise in eternal perfection. You will come to understand that attaining the divine perfection is the primary purpose of all of God's creations.

> 'God is primal reality in the spirit world; God is the source of truth in the mind spheres; God overshadows all throughout the material realms. To all created intelligences God is a personality, and to the universe of universes he is the First Source and Center of eternal reality. God is neither manlike nor machinelike. The First Father is universal spirit, eternal truth, infinite reality, and father personality.' (*Urantia*)

"The existence of God can never be proven through scientific or philosophical means. God can only be realized through experiential means. As the *Urantia Book* declares:

> 'Those who know God have experienced the fact of his presence; such God knowing mortals hold in their personal experience the only positive proof of the existence of the

living God which one human being can offer to another. The existence of God is utterly beyond all possibility of demonstration except for the contact between the God-consciousness of the human mind and the God-presence of the Thought Adjuster that indwells the mortal intellect and is bestowed upon man as the free gift of the Universal Father.'

"Even here, in the world of Spirit, there exists no proof of an existence of a Deity. All that is Spirit is aware of the Universal Father through the realization of the Love that permeates all things. It is impossible for mortal man to approach the Spirit of God and maintain his/her existence. God's glory and spiritual brilliance is beyond approach by any material being, where God is only known through Its unconditional Love. Even here and now, in this world of Spirit, the Love that is God can only be experienced to the degree of one's attunement to Divine Consciousness."

"If there are degrees of God's Love, why is it only limited in the material world?"

"It's a matter of vibration! The human body cannot entertain such a high degree of consciousness or Love without bursting at the seams. Likewise, here in our spiritual realm, consciousness of Love cannot fall below the level of enlightenment because of the same vibratory restrictions. Should Spirit's vibration fall below the level of enlightenment, it will materialize in the objective world."

"So there can never be 'hate' here, only degrees of Love?"

"There can never be 'hate' anywhere, Hans, because hate is a judgment, not a state of consciousness. There are only degrees of Love. Even the lowest realization of Love exists in every material entity, whether animate or inanimate. It has to be that way because Love is everywhere. 'God is spirit - spirit personality; man is also spirit - potential spirit personality.' (*Urantia*) If you replace the term spirit with Love, you have: God is Love - Love personality; man is also Love - potential Love personality.

'(God the Father) is defined as consisting in spirit and manifesting himself to the universe as love. Therefore, in all his personal relation with the creature personalities of the universe, the First Source and Center is always and consistently a loving Father. God is a Father in the highest sense of the term. He is eternally motivated by the perfect idealism of divine love, and that tender nature  finds  its strongest expression and greatest satisfaction in loving and being loved.

'As this love-comprehension of Deity finds spiritual expression in the lives of God-knowing mortals, there are yielded the fruits of divinity: intellectual peace, social progress, moral satisfaction, spiritual joy, and cosmic wisdom. The advanced mortals...have learned that love is the greatest thing in the universe - and they know that God is love...Love is the desire to do good to others.

'All true love is from God, and man receives the divine affection as he himself bestows this love upon his fellows. Love is dynamic. It can never be captured; it is alive, free, thrilling, and always moving. Man can never take the love of the Father and imprison it within his heart. The Father's love can become real to mortal man only by passing through that man's personality as he in turn bestows this love upon his fellows. The great circuit of love is from the Father, through sons to brothers, and hence to the Supreme. The love of the Father appears in the mortal personality by the ministry of the indwelling Adjuster. Such a God-knowing son reveals this love to his universe brethren, and this fraternal affection is the essence of the love of the Supreme.' (*Urantia Book*)

"As you can see Hans, Love is the answer to the question, 'Who/ What is God?' In fact, Love is the answer to all questions! Here in the realm of Spirit we continually realize this Love just as you are realizing it now. It's always Love. Every question has its foundation in Love, hence, every answer comes from that same awareness."

"Yes Teacher, I can feel Love's brilliance, I can hear Love's soothing chant. I understand that at the heart of every why, if, and when, lies the undercurrent of Love. *Being*, therefore, is quite simply Love!"

"And as you awaken to even greater Love, you will find Love is all there is. Once one embraces the Divine Covenant that Love is here, Love is there, Love is everywhere, only then will one know God. And only then will one embark on a continuous journey of elevating their vibration, resulting in even greater conscious awakening and divinely inspired creation."

"So I will continue to spiritually awaken for eternity growing closer and closer to All That Is until I return home to The One?"

"Yes Hans. As you must realize now, 'Death is not real, even in the Relative sense - it is but Birth to a new life - and You shall go on, and on, and on, to higher and still higher planes of life, for eons upon eons of time. The Universe is your home, and you shall explore its farthest recesses before the end of Time. You are dwelling in the Infinite Mind of THE ALL, and your possibilities and opportunities are infinite, both in time and space. And at the end of the Grand Cycle of Eons, when THE ALL shall draw back into itself all of its creations - you will go gladly, for you will then be able to know the Whole Truth of *Being* At One with THE ALL...And, in the meantime, rest calm and serene - you are safe and protected by the Infinite Power of the FATHER-MOTHER MIND.'" (Kybalion)

"Dear Teacher, is there any way you can describe the journey?"

"Your journey here is difficult to explain and, therefore, even more difficult to understand, especially for newly transformed personalities like you. Please realize that I will attempt to describe the process in its simplicity so it will be easier to comprehend. Understand this to be a high- level, strategic description of a spiritual morphing that will take countless eons to complete."

"I understand, Teacher."

"After one dies and their soul has made sufficient spiritual progress during their mortal years they will be destined for further spiritual growth. If one has not made sufficient spiritual progress, they will reincarnate to the mortal sphere and continue that cycle until they attain the sufficient spiritual growth.

"Their journey is a continuous progression of spiritual evolution, or awakening as I like to describe it, evolving through several stages specifically designed to prepare the soul for its ultimate perfection and never ending service by developing wisdom and love while coming into greater alignment with the Divine.

"After death, one's initial ascension is to, what *The Urantia Book* calls, the Morontia Mansions, which is a temporary state between the objective and subjective realms, where one's soul takes on a redefined form in preparation for continuing its spiritual journey. Here *Beings* undergo a gradual transformation that frees them from their material restrictions while presenting them with higher spiritual realities. Significant learning and growth takes place in the Morontia Mansions, enabling souls to overcome residual materialism, increase their understanding of divine truths, and strengthen their understanding and relationship with their internal Spirit. This is, essentially, a state of healing while laying the groundwork for greater spiritual service.

"Once this initial training has been completed, the journey continues through a series of higher levels, each ascending level offers more profound insights and responsibilities. Advancing through these stages, the soul becomes aware of greater spiritual realities as it continues to shed remnants of its material existence, continuing its deeper understanding of the Divine, while increasing its ability to express divine love and come into greater alignment with God's will.

"After completing its Morontia training in the local universe, it ascends to the super-universe, where countless local universes reside. Here *Being* becomes aware of greater cosmic realities and more advanced forms of service. As *Being* nears the halfway point of its journey back to the Divine, the super-universes prepare *Being* for the final stages of ascension to the central universe, which is a place of perfect and eternal creation. Within the central universe exist billions of perfect worlds, each offering further experiences and challenges to continue perfecting *Being*. Here *Being* becomes fully aligned with the Universal Father, while attaining spiritual perfection. This is one of the final preparatory steps before a union with the Divine can take place on Paradise.

"Paradise is the culmination of the *Being's* journey. It is the center of all creation and the place where it unites with the Divine in perfect love and understanding. Here Being joins other perfect *Beings* and participates in the unfolding of God's will throughout all creation.

"Each *Being* contributes to the realization of God's plan throughout the universes, bringing all creation closer to Divine Oneness. The Divine is an eternal state of *Being* in complete alignment with the Universal Father. This marks the final destination of a long and transformative journey through many complex levels of existence."

"I noticed that the soul was no longer mentioned and seemed to be replaced by *Being*. What happens to the soul?'

"The soul is actually a creation of Spirit, just as are all material things. Through the growth of consciousness and the return to Divine Source, all creations of Spirit return to their creator, just as Spirit ultimately returns to its creator, First Cause or Source or All That Is, or Divine *Being*, or God, however you wish to identify It. *Being* is, therefore, the original state of everything, the energy from which everything was created and to which everything will ultimately return."

"Will Love stay with me throughout this process?"

"Love is the process, Hans. Love is the process!"

As Teacher was explaining things to me, a giant hologram appeared before me playing one reel of experiences after another. I found myself watching some and entering the doorway to others. In some I was rich while in others I was poor. There were lifetimes of need and wants, yet others filled with an overabundance of wealth. I was hated, I was loved, I was male, I was female, I was intelligent and I was of poor intellect Yet each experience led me to a higher consciousness of the Divine, each experience awakened me more to who I really am.

I melded with the consciousness of a rock, lying for centuries on one place before being somehow jostled to another place. I melded with an insect whose momentary life was cut short by the hoof of some large animal, I understood a blade of grass and that dying leaf high in a tree ready to embark on its final journey to the ground and become the fertilizer for plants to come. Then I melded with a flower and watched as I was picked to beautify some grateful person's home.

As I moved in and out of experiences, every one left me with a higher conscious awareness enabling me to tap further and further into Divine Love. Every instant passing through my experience offered a greater insight to the Oneness of all things. Every instant brought a little more love than the moment before it. It took me lifetimes to realize that life was one big learning experience designed to bring me closer to the Divine.

I traveled throughout this planet from the highest mountains to the deepest seas learning through experiences along the way. And when there was nothing more to learn, I traveled the universe from galaxy to galaxy, continually growing my consciousness, the lessons to be learned weren't always clear or easily understood, but, after countless experiences, I learned to look for them.

That must have been the turning point, for once I understood that my material experiences were not a playground of events passing before me, but a series of continuous opportunities from which to learn and grow a higher consciousness. I began to focus on service and helping others without regard to myself. I came to realize my neighbor was just as important to my material existence as I was to his. Most importantly, I learned to recognize and embrace the Spirit within everything I encountered and everyone I met.

I came to know my Spirit. I came to know that internal divinity existing within everyone. I came to know who I really am. As I grew in Love so did my soul and with an ever-increasing awareness, my internal Spirit presented itself. It was then that I entered the enlightened worlds of material perfection. Here everyone and everything was respected and loved. Life's purpose was fully understood raising the consciousness of things, individuals, the planet, the galaxy and the universe. Divine interconnectedness was fully realized. I finally understood Teacher when he said, "Love is the process."

When I finally returned to Teacher embossed in his entire splendor, I knew what would come next. My training in the local universe was complete. Beckoning me to follow him, we took one final journey through the universe, re-visiting my countless experiences before coming to rest on an enlightened planet in the Andromeda Galaxy. Walking through its glowing grass and fragrant flowers we came to a marble castle glowing in light.

"Our journey ends here," Teacher proclaimed.

"I know and I am forever grateful for your guidance and insights. I will remember and love you forever." We embraced one final time as our essence melded into one brilliant ball of light energy that grew brighter and brighter. Eventually we separated and I headed to the castle. Teacher, I knew, was already on his way to guide another soul through the un-assuredness and pitfalls of the journey towards spiritual awareness. I stepped on my bridge crossing the castle's moat, realizing many other souls were entering the castle as well. It was here where I would remove my soul overcoat and let my Spirit within emerge.

# Chapter 21

## The No Thing

*"And just as the shadow can never be the light, the story I tell can never be the Supreme Truth, but perhaps through these pages there can be a momentary taste of the elixir of eternity."*

Kagan

As I cross the moat and enter the castle, I find myself standing before a giant altar whose makeup reaches to the highest levels of the room. It is of white marble, as streams of lights dance across the altar creating hues of indigo, mauve and bright gold. It is a display far surpassing the great Independence Day fireworks at the Hudson River's entrance to New York harbor. While this great display of light dances before me, I am aware that before me lies the gateway to the great emptiness of the Absolute.

As I prepare to enter the void I realize that in order to progress to the super-universe I must leave behind all my earthly attachment including my soul. By entering the void I will travel beyond space and time and, this time, I will travel beyond creation. This is the world of non-existence, where the absence of light and sound and *Beingness* will prepare me to return to my pure Spirit Self. Within the Nothingness I am preparing to become the Allness. To understand its purpose, I must look beyond the basic understanding of "nothing" as a mere absence of things or emptiness. Spiritually, "no thing" suggests an intense state of *Being*, a space of unlimited potential, and a source for all existence.

Here the extremes come together to form a Spiritual Wholeness that will take me on my final path to the Divine. Here I am nothing and everything. I am a beggar and a king. I am a tyrant and a saint. Here I come to understand that the Divine is everything and nothing. To get here I needed to be born and die many times. I am the suffering. I am the grace. I am the truth. I am the play and the actor and the director and the audience.

Once I enter here, I will not return. My journey will continue until I'm reunited with the Divine Oneness. Before the altar appears a giant throne of welcoming. It will take me to where I need to go, where I need to be. Teacher has prepared me well for this moment. I climb the twelve marble steps to the throne and fall to my knees, proclaiming:

*"Divine Presence, Source of All Being,*

*I come before You now, stripped of all that I am, willing to surrender my very essence into the vastness of Your boundless embrace. In this sacred moment, I release all thoughts, all fears, all identities that cling to my soul, letting them dissolve into the nothingness that is You.*

*Guide me, O Infinite One, into the heart of the void where silence reigns, where the only sound is the whisper of Your breath upon my spirit. May I find the courage to let go of the illusions I have built, the stories I have lived, the desires I have chased. For in this sacred void, there is no past, no future, no time, no space—only the pure, undiluted presence of Your love.*

*As I step into this abyss, I trust in Your eternal light to guide me, even as it disappears from my sight. I surrender my need for understanding, my need for control, my need for anything other than Your holy will. In this emptiness, may I find fullness; in this silence, may I hear Your voice; in this darkness, may I see Your face.*

*I am ready to be undone, to be unmade, to be reborn in the fires of Your nothingness. Let me become the void, the vessel, the sacred space where You dwell. Let me lose myself completely, that I may find myself fully in You.*

*Take me, O Divine Mystery, into the depths of Your unfathomable love. Let me float in the stillness of Your peace, rest in the tranquility of Your being, and dissolve into the oneness of Your essence. For I am Yours, now and forevermore.*

*In the void, I find You. In the nothingness, I am found. Amen."*

One final flashback crossed my mind, or should I say "flashnow" since linear time-space does not exist in the Spirit world. It was Teacher who described a soul to me.

"The soul does not reside within the individual person, rather the person resides in the soul. It is the soul that through contraction and expansion creates physical personalities. These expansions and contractions, much like an electrical transformer, contracts, or slows down, the vibration energy to create form and expands, or increases the vibration energy, to bring the physical back into the Spiritual. As Emerson stated in the "Oversoul:"

'...within man is the soul of the whole; the wise silence; the universal beauty, to  which every part and particle is equally related; the eternal One..

A man is the facade of a temple wherein all wisdom and good abide. What we commonly call man, the eating, drinking, planting, counting man, does not, as we know him, represent himself, but misrepresents himself. Him we do not respect, but the soul, whose organ he is, would he let it appear through his action, would make our knees bend. When it breathes through his intellect, it is genius; when it breathes through his will, it is virtue; when it flows through his affection, it is love...We see the world piece by piece, as the sun, the moon, the animal, the tree; but the whole, of which these are the shining parts, is the soul.'

"This cycle, of the soul contracting and expanding, continues many times creating many lifetime experiences. As the soul cycles through these lifetimes it passes through stages of Nothingness during which vibration levels are decreased and increased. The gestation process in the womb before physical birth is one such example. The return to Spirit after the physical body dies is another. In the presence of Now, these changes in vibration occur instantly, while these changes in vibration can last months or years in the world of form, as evidenced by the nine month birthing process.

"But the soul itself goes through a similar process. It exists within a larger Spiritual body that Emerson calls the 'Over-soul, within which every man's particular being is contained and made one with all other.' It is here where the return to Divine Oneness takes place."

Without hesitation, I take my place on the throne and, after one final look, I close my eyes and empty my mind and allow darkness to slowly overtake me. As a final Ernest Holmes verse leaves the remnants of my mind, I enter the great unknown.

> When death shall come
> And the spirit, freed, shall mount the air,
> And wander afar in that great no-where,
> It shall go as it came,
> Freed from sorrow, sin and shame;
> And naked and bare, through the upper air
> Shall go alone to that great no-where.
> Hinder not its onward way,
> Grieve not o'er its form of clay,
> For the spirit, freed now from clod,
> Shall go alone to meet its God. (Holmes)

I am in a sea of Love, ebbing and flowing as Divine Energy enters and leaves. I am an integral part of All There Is, for without me the Wholeness could not exist. My personality is still with me, although I see things and experience things quite differently than when I was in human form.

An infinite number of experiences were made available to me, in preparation for this moment. All I needed to do was to will them into existence. These experiences, whether short or long, were each created with a consciousness of Love; each a stepping- stone leading me to the great void of Spiritual incarnation.

I found myself in this same void before I entered the world of form when I needed to slow my vibration. At that time the nothingness was the place where the birth of material form took place; it still is the place of the great creative womb. Only this time I am returning to the Spirit I Am. As Sunshine Michelle Coleman describes, "The space of the shadows and darkness is fertile ground where creativity and new beginnings gestate and are born." Here I wait in silence, bathed in Love as the return to my spiritual roots awaits me.

Within this Nothingness lies the accumulation of all that could be. It is the source from which all forms, structures, and beings emerge; it is a space of pure potential, where all possibilities exist in a dormant state, while maintaining the balance between various cosmic realities. It ensures that the universe operates in harmony, integrating the finite and infinite, the material and spiritual, and the perfect and the imperfect. In this cosmic womb exists the source of all divine action, a treasure of unrealized potential waiting to be realized.

Ernest Holmes describes "no thing" as the infinite potential from which all things emerge. It's not a void but a fertile ground of possibility. When we meditate on nothingness, we're not seeking an absence but rather tuning into the source from which everything originates. This source, often referred to as the Universal Mind or Divine Consciousness, is a state of pure potentiality. It is the unmanifest, the space before form, the silence before sound.

The purpose of this spiritual "no thing" is multifaceted. First, it serves as a reminder of our inherent connection to the Divine. By contemplating nothingness, we recognize that the essence of our being is not confined to the physical world. Our true nature is boundless, timeless, and infinite. This realization can be profoundly liberating, as it frees us from the limitations and attachments of the material world. We begin to see ourselves not as isolated entities but as integral parts of a vast, interconnected whole.

Thomas Troward, another influential figure in the New Thought movement, suggests that nothingness is not a barren void but a dynamic field of energy waiting to be shaped by our consciousness. When we engage with this field through focused intention and clear visualization, we become co-creators with the Divine, bringing forth new expressions of life and love.

Emma Curtis Hopkins taught that the "no thing" is a sacred space where we can commune with the Divine and receive guidance. For Hopkins, the purpose of nothingness was to serve as a gateway to deeper spiritual understanding and personal transformation. By entering this space, we can release old patterns, heal past wounds, and awaken to our true purpose.

While these mystics taught the purpose of the spiritual "no thing" is to reconnect us with the infinite source of all existence, it also serves as a reminder of our true nature, a space of potential, and a foundation for creativity and transformation. By embracing nothingness, we surpass the limitations of the material world and open ourselves to the boundless possibilities of the Divine. This journey into the "no thing" is not about escaping reality but about deepening our understanding of it and our place within it. It's an invitation to live with greater awareness, intention, and alignment with the universal flow of life.

Here in the No Thing I am raising my vibration to enter the Over-soul, the true *Being* of Spirit. Out of the Nothingness will rise a divinely blessed personality fully prepared to continue its journey to Divine Oneness. A single ray of light, brighter than any I had yet experienced, pierced through the darkness alerting me that my wait was almost done. Within this single ray I found a higher love and peace I had yet known. Gradually more light appeared showering me with yet even greater love and peace, until I became Love and Peace.

When the Light had overcome the Void, I found myself standing before a landscape of snow-covered mountains reaching high above the clouds. Standing before them were several figures dressed in pure white robes. While I didn't recognize them, their love and joy penetrated everything that lay before me. Sparkles of the shiniest silver floated around the air, penetrating everything with unimaginable Love.

They are Supreme *Beings* of pure Spirit welcoming me to the world of the Oversoul. All attachment to my previous existence was released only the quest for greater Love remains. Here, in this enraptured whiteness, I will come to know the divinity of the Absolute. Here, in this heavenly place of wonderment, I will let go of the last vestiges of my earthly existence, my soul.

"Rays from several of the (*Beings'*) hands reach out and join with my fingertips. I become one with their light, but oh, I want you to know, you must understand, that they are so most thankfully not me. They are so much more than me. Through them, I am becoming the first impulse of the Divine Source: Spirit. From pure soul I am becoming pure Spirit. And, as Spirit, I will leave the system of earth and all its heavens and go to another Universe. I have cast off my earthly disguise, my life, my drama, my music; everything is being left behind, even my soul.

"And as I go on to another Universe, flickering as a beam of light into the  unknown, flickering as a flame of pure Spirit in and out of consciousness, flickering from being to non-being and back again, as I do so, I ask only (this one thing:) ...keep listening for my voice, and always, always and forever remember my love." (Kagan)

# Epilogue

As I sit here, reflecting on the journey that has brought me to this moment, I am filled with a profound sense of gratitude and awe. The path I've walked—one of questioning, seeking, and discovering—has been transformative, yet I know in my heart it is just the beginning. I've come to understand that spirituality is not a destination but an unfolding process, a journey of becoming, of shedding layers, and of revealing the truth of who we are beneath the illusion of separation.

Throughout this book, I've shared the milestones of my own journey—how I moved from a place of uncertain belief to a more grounded, living truth that continually evolves. This evolution, however, is not something that happens in a vacuum. It is interwoven with the teachings of those who have walked this path before me: Ernest Holmes, Ralph Waldo Emerson, Thomas Troward, Emma Curtis Hopkins, and others who have dedicated their lives to the study of the deeper, unseen truths of existence. Their insights have been like beacons, guiding me through the fog of confusion, showing me that there is a deeper intelligence at play in this world, a Divine Mind that we are all part of.

One of the key revelations I have come to understand is the profound interconnectedness of all things. The idea of Universal Oneness is not just an abstract, philosophical concept; it is a living, breathing truth that we must experience, integrate, and practice in our daily lives. When I first encountered the idea, it felt lofty, even beyond my grasp. But as I delved deeper into the writings of Ernest Holmes, I began to see it in everything—in the quiet moments of stillness, in the energy that pulses through the world, and even in the struggle and suffering. Holmes often spoke of the Law of Mind, which governs not only our thoughts but the very nature of reality itself. This law, he said, operates like a mirror, reflecting back to us what we project into it. In this way, our thoughts and beliefs shape our experience of the world. And yet, even more profoundly, they shape the very essence of who we are *Becoming*.

I learned that enlightenment isn't some distant goal we must strive toward, but rather the natural unfolding of our consciousness as we align ourselves with the Divine. To live in alignment with this Universal Mind requires us to recognize our own divinity, to see ourselves not as separate from God, but as expressions of God's own infinite potential. This realization, though it may come in flashes, is not always easy to sustain. The world, with its noise, distractions, and conditioned beliefs, constantly pulls us away from this awareness. But the more we practice—whether through meditation, prayer, mindfulness, or simply being present—the more we begin to see the truth of this interconnectedness in all things.

One of the most striking truths I have discovered along the way is the Law of Vibration. The universe is not a static place. It is dynamic, alive, and constantly in motion. Every thought, every feeling, every action emits a vibration, a frequency that ripples outward and interacts with the world. Emerson captured this beautifully when he spoke about the "invisible world." What we cannot see, he argued, is just as real—and perhaps more real—than what we can touch or measure. The vibrations we send out shape the fabric of our reality, and they are felt not just by us, but by the very fabric of existence itself. It is this law that connects us to one another and to the universe, that reminds us that we are never alone in our thoughts or experiences.

Emma Curtis Hopkins, in her writing, often emphasized the power of love as the highest and most transformative vibration in the universe. Love, she said, is the Divine energy that permeates all things, that binds everything together, and that has the power to heal and uplift. She taught that by aligning ourselves with the energy of love, we become more attuned to the Divine presence within and around us. This energy is not bound by time or space; it transcends the limitations of our physical bodies and connects us to the eternal. In learning to love ourselves and others with an unconditional, all-encompassing love, we open ourselves to the infinite flow of Divine wisdom and creativity.

Yet, the challenge is not simply understanding these teachings intellectually but living them. As I began to put my beliefs into practice, I found that true spirituality isn't about adhering to a set of dogmas or rituals, but about living in harmony with the Universal Laws of Mind, Vibration, and Love. It is about choosing, moment by moment, to embody the truth of our interconnectedness. It is about recognizing that every action, every thought, every interaction sends ripples into the universe that will return to us, shaped by our own energy and vibration.

And in this journey of *Becoming*, I have learned that there is no "end point." Enlightenment is not a final destination where we can say we have arrived, but a state of *Being* that is continually unfolding. It is a practice of being present, of continually choosing to see the Divine in all things, and of trusting that the path we are on is one of growth, expansion, and transformation. The journey is as sacred as the destination, and the destination itself is a never-ending revelation of the Divine.

In closing, I want to share a thought that has resonated deeply with me, from Ralph Waldo Emerson. He once wrote, "The soul is not in the body, but the body is in the soul." This profound statement speaks to the core of what I've come to understand. Our true essence is not the temporary, physical self, but the eternal soul that animates it. This soul is part of the Divine Oneness, indivisible and infinite. It is this soul that leads us toward enlightenment, toward the recognition that we are not separate from God, but are God's expression in the world.

As I close this chapter of my journey and prepare to embark on the next, I carry with me the wisdom and love of those who have come before me, and the knowledge that I am not alone. We are all part of this great, universal web, each of us an expression of the Divine. And though the journey may be long and full of twists and turns, I know that it is a journey worth taking, for it is the journey back to the truth of who we truly are.

And so, I step forward—knowing that each moment is an opportunity to *Believe*, to *Become*, and to *Be*.

# About the Author

Hans Benes is a spiritual writer, metaphysical thinker, and lifelong seeker whose work explores the evolving relationship between belief, consciousness, and Divine reality. With a grounding in the teachings of Science of Mind and inspired by spiritual luminaries such as Ernest Holmes, Ralph Waldo Emerson, Thomas Troward, and Emma Curtis Hopkins, Hans Benes writes with the intention of awakening others to their innate spiritual authority and the sacred unity that underlies all existence.

Their writing is both reflective and revelatory, shaped by years of inquiry into the nature of consciousness, the law of vibration, and the energetic essence of love as expressions of the Divine. With a degree from New York University and a deep commitment to critical thinking, Hans Benes bridges intellectual insight with spiritual intuition, offering readers a space to explore their own soul's unfolding.

*Believing, Becoming, Being* is the third installment in a growing body of spiritual work. In his earlier books, *The God Dichotomy* and *The God Dichotomy: Letting Go*, Hans Benes examined the inner conflict between inherited images of a judgmental God and the deeper truth of a loving, unifying Presence. Those works laid the foundation for this latest offering, which moves beyond deconstruction into a personal and practical expression of spiritual embodiment.

At the heart of Hans Benes' message is the conviction that we are not separate from the Divine but are individualized expressions of It, unfolding into greater awareness. Through writing, teaching, and spiritual dialogue, Hans Benes invites others to discover the Divine within themselves and to live from that place of wholeness, presence, and love.

To learn more, visit Hans Benes' official website at hansbenes.com where you'll find additional writings, updates, and reflections. You can also connect through Facebook and Instagram.

*"What lies behind us and what lies before us are tiny matters compared to what lies within us."*

—Ralph Waldo Emerson

*"The Truth is not something I found—it is something I remembered. And in remembering, I became free."*

—Hans Benes

# Bibliography

Adyashanti. *Resurrecting Jesus*. Boulder: Sounds True, Inc., 2014.

Addington, Jack and Cornelia. *The Joy of Meditation*. Camarillo, CA.:DeVorss & Company.

Atkinson, William Walker. *Thought Vibration or the Law of Attraction in the Thought World*. Las Vegas: Digitalized by Watchmaker Publishing, 2015.

Beach, Jane. *Remembering Who I Am*. Portland: Kenos Press, 2015.

Butterworth, Eric. *Spiritual Economics*. Unity Village, Missouri: Unity House, 2001.

Cayce, Hugh, Lynn. *Jesus' Course in Miracles*. Course in Miracles Society, 2000.

Coelho, Paulo. *The Alchemist*. San Francisco: Harper Collins, 1994.

Coleman, Sunshine Michelle. "Light Within the Shadows." *Science of Mind*, Vol. 96, No. 5, May 2023, pp. 28-30.

Cooper, David, Rabbi. *God is a Verb*. New York: Riverhead Books, 1997.

Goldsmith, Joel S. *Living the Infinite Way*. Longboat Key: Acropolis Books, 1961.

Goldsmith, Joel S. *Practicing the Presence*. Longboat Key: Acropolis Books, 1958.

Goddard, Neville. *The Power of Imagination*. New York: Penguin Group, 2015.

Hawkins, David, R. *In the World, But Not Of It*. New York: Hay House, 2023.

Holmes, Ernest. *Can We Talk to God?*. Deerfield Beach: Health Communications, 1992.

Holmes, Ernest. *This Thing Called You*. New York: Dodd, Mead, 1948.

Holmes, Ernest. *The Science of Mind*. New York: Penguin Putnam Inc., 1938.

Howard, David. *In This Moment*. Dallas: Wisdom House Books, 2007.

Howard, David, Reverend. "Embracing Wholeness." December 3, 2023. Center for Spiritual Living, Parker, CO.

Howard, David, Reverend. "Recognizing Wholeness: Seeing the Good in All." December 10, 2023. Center for Spiritual Living. Parker, CO.

Kagan, Annie. The Afterlife of Billy Fingers. Charlottesville, VA: Hampton Roads Publishing, 2013.

Khechog, Nawang. *Awakening Kindness*. New York: Atria Books, 2010.

Noe, Karen. *We Consciousness*. New York City: Hay House, 2018.

Nepo, Mark. *The Book of Awakening*. Newburyport: Red Wheel, 2020.

Nepo, Mark. *The Book of Soul*. New York: St. Martin's Publishing Group, 2020.

Osho. *Zen Tarot*. New York: St. Martin's Press, 1994.

Perry, Robert. *The Elder Brother*. Sedona: Robert Perry, 1990.

Richardson, Christopher David. *The Complete Gnostic Gospels*. Troutdale, 2023.

Singer, Michael A. *Living Untethered*. Oakland: New Harbinger Publications, 2022.

Starcke, Walter. *It's All God*. Boerne, Texas: Guadalupe Press, 1998.

Stewart, Raymond P. *Living as God*. Vancouver: Namaste Publishing, 2004.

Thich Nhat Hanh. *Living Buddha*, Living Christ. New York: Berkley Publishing Group, 1995.

Three Initiates. *The Kybalion*. Chicago: The Yogi Publication Society, 1908.

Tolle, Eckhart. *The Power of Now*. Novato, CA: New World Library, 1997.

Trine, Ralph Waldo. *In Tune With the Infinite*. United States: Sublime Books, 2014.

Twyman, James. *The Kabbalah Code*. New York City: Hay House, 2009.

Walsch, Neale Donald. *Conversations With God Book 2.*

Wells, Sarah. "What did Eckhart Tolle mean by, 'The secret to life is to die before you die?'" https://www.quora.com/What-did-Eckhart-Tolle-mean-by-The-secret-to-life-is-to-die-before-you-die.May, 2024.

www.ingramcontent.com/pod-product-compliance
Lightning Source LLC
Chambersburg PA
CBHW020756310726
48969CB00002B/571